THE LAYMAN'S BOOK
OF REVELATIONS

B.J. Corey

Order this book online at www.trafford.com
or email orders@trafford.com

Most Trafford titles are also available at major online book retailers.

Note for Librarians: A cataloguing record for this book is available from Library
and Archives Canada at www.collectionscanada.ca/amicus/index-e.html

Printed in Victoria, BC, Canada.

ISBN: 978-1-4251-8532-9 (Soft)

*We at Trafford believe that it is the responsibility of us all, as both individuals
and corporations, to make choices that are environmentally and socially sound.
You, in turn, are supporting this responsible conduct each time you purchase a
Trafford book, or make use of our publishing services. To find out how you are
helping, please visit www.trafford.com/responsiblepublishing.html*

*Our mission is to efficiently provide the world's finest, most comprehensive
book publishing service, enabling every author to experience success.
To find out how to publish your book, your way, and have it available
worldwide, visit us online at www.trafford.com*

Trafford rev. 7/16/2009

 www.trafford.com

North America & international
toll-free: 1 888 232 4444 (USA & Canada)
phone: 250 383 6864 ♦ fax: 250 383 6804 ♦ email: info@trafford.com

FORWARD

While doing preparatory research in order to teach a class in my local church on the book of revelations, I studied what several noted scholars had written on the subject. During the course of this research, I soon came to a couple of conclusions that were somewhat astonishing to me.

First off, while I was expecting some minor disagreements between these learned men, I was not prepared for so many opposing interpretations of the events and visions recorded in the original scripture.

Where two different explanations of a particular portion of text are diametrically opposed, only one can possibly be divinely inspired. The dilemma here is: How do you know which one? The possibility also surfaces that neither is divinely inspired. What does one do?

My approach to that problem has always been to first ask myself: "What is God trying to tell me?" If the answer is not readily apparent, my next step is to prayerfully ask God: "What are you trying to tell me?" This system has never failed me. You may say, "why not just skip step one and go directly to step two?" I believe that God wants us to exercise our own cognitive powers to the best of our ability in order to better understand his perfect love, his character, and his will for our lives. He is, however, always waiting in the wings for those moments when our own feeble intellects fail us.

For centuries scholars have spent countless hours, even decades, trying to unravel the unfathomable mysteries contained within the book of revelations. To what purpose? I am certain that in due time, as it suits HIS purpose, God will reveal these mysteries to all believers. Until that time, we can only speculate on most of it's deepest mysteries. While each of us tends to speculate in our own thoughts, we should never offer these speculations to the world as absolute truths, as some have done.

In this book, I have ignored the more abstract explanations of these expositors, arriving at my conclusions through much prayer and study, always interpreting God's message as literal. I believe with all my being that God said what he meant and meant what he said! He has absolutely no need for an interpreter. If I had to declare my most outstanding trait as a bible teacher, it would have to be my unwavering faith, not only in the fact that the bible was divinely inspired in it's original writings, but also that God, who foresees all future, was equally divinely inspiring to those who assembled and published the King James Bible that I use today.

Furthermore, I claim no privileged understanding of scripture. While, as I said before, I put a great deal of prayer and study into writing this book, the thoughts and explanations are my own, and not to be construed as divinely inspired. Infallibility is the exclusive domain of Jehovah God.

Secondly, all the material I read seemed to be aimed at the serious scholar rather than the layman. There was little fluidity to the text, and the writing was saturated with theological jargon that would have the average layperson frequently reaching for a dictionary.

There were also numerous references to other works by other scholars so that in order to get the full knowledge of the material presented, one would need access to a seminary library.

While I realized there is a definite need for such writings as those that I had read, I thought to myself, there ought to be a book that was comfortable for the layperson to read. It was then that the light turned on. I thought to myself, you're doing the research anyway, why don't you write it?

I immediately began to conjure up all sorts of excuses. After all these were exhausted, I still could not convince myself that it was not a good idea, but I decided to relegate it to my list of things to do sometime in the far distant future. (As a sixty nine year old, I don't even have a far distant future!)

2

As our class progressed, I became more enthused, and I finally reached a point where it became almost an obsession. From our class discussions and my preparatory research, I began to distinguish between the actual truths of the book of revelations, and the most popular misconceptions of modern man, many of which I had been taught and consequently believed since early childhood. Many of these preconceived notions were hard to let go of. One of the hardest things for a person my age to do is admit that something they believed for so many years is wrong. I am certain that some readers will, as I did, have certain preconceived ideas. All that I request is that you read this book prayerfully with an open mind, considering that some of your ideas might be wrong. I, at the same time, honor your right to disagree with some of my explanations. My goal is not to re-educate you, but that in reading this book the magnitude of the prophesies in the book of Revelations will be brought to the forefront of your consciousness, at least for a moment, and preferably, for the rest of your life.

Once I had gotten past the mental block, the material fairly flowed. While I would not be so bold as to say that God gave me specific instructions to write this book, I could feel his presence as I labored over the work. It is my earnest prayer that he be pleased with the results.

ON THE BOOK OF REVELATIONS

Before we get into the study of the book of revelations, I would make the reader aware of two important concepts.

1. Do not try to picture the events in chronological order. Some of the events follow each other, but not all. The text jumps back and forth in time.

2. Do not try to explain supernatural events of the Bible in natural ways. As an example, when the text says the elements will melt with fervent heat, do not picture this as a nuclear holocaust, rather picture it as the fiery breath of an angry God.

THE ORIGIN OF THE BOOK

The book of revelations was the last book of the New Testament to be written. The date of its writing can be almost certainly identified as 95 or 96 A.D., and its very existence is a remarkable work of God.

During the reign of Emperor Domitian (81-96 A.D.) the apostle John, who was then the pastor of the church at Ephesus, was banished to the isle of Patmos. Patmos was a tiny forbidding island in the Aegean Sea containing a penal colony that operated mines, utilizing inmate labor.

While John might possibly have received some special consideration, I feel that is extremely unlikely. It is more probable that he was forced to work in the mines. The Roman Emperor Domitian was noted for severely punishing anyone who disagreed with his policies and this would surely include the Christians, as one of his foremost policies was that he should be referred to as a god, a policy I am certain that John was openly and vigorously opposed to.

On top of the terrible conditions under which prisoners were forced to work in these mines, John would probably have been between ninety and one hundred years old, possibly even older. It readily becomes apparent that John was purposely "kept" by God so that he could write the book. I believe that Christ makes reference to this divine keeping of John in the gospel of John, chapter twenty one, verses twenty through twenty three.

20 Then Peter, turning about seeth the disciple whom Jesus loved (John) following; which also leaned on his breast at supper and said, Lord which is he that betrayeth thee?

21 Peter seeing him saith to Jesus, Lord, and what shall this man do?

22 Jesus saith unto him, if I will that he tarry till I come, what is that to thee? Follow thou me.

23 Then went this saying abroad among the brethren that that disciple should not die; yet Jesus said not unto him, he shall not die; but if I will that he tarry till I come what is that to thee?

John identifies himself more than once in the scripture as "the disciple whom Jesus loved". I do not believe he was claiming any special status, but that he was simply testifying to the fact that he knew the Master loved him; much in the same sense that we sing the hymn: "Jesus loves me this I know".

What did Jesus mean when he said that John would "tarry till I come"? He was not speaking of his second coming to the whole world, but of his private appearance to John to give him the revelation!

Upon the assassination of Domitian in 96 A.D., John was released from his captivity and returned to Ephesus where he published his work.

THE BOOK OF REVELATIONS

CHAPTER 1

1. The revelation of Jesus Christ, which God gave unto him, to show unto his servants things which must surely come to pass; and sent and signified it by his angel unto his servant John.
2. Who bare record of the word of God, and of the testimony of Jesus Christ, and of all things he saw.

John immediately begins by identifying the author as God, through Christ, given to John through an angel sent by Christ.

I would like to make one point perfectly clear at the onset. While the apostle John is generally credited as the author of the book of revelations, it's author is in fact, God himself. While John performed the mechanics of the writing, God provided one hundred percent of the thought. When writing about scripture, some scholars tend to consider or interject the mindset of the writer at the time of writing. If all scripture is one hundred percent divinely inspired, (as I am absolutely sure it is), then the private thoughts or the mindset of the writer have absolutely no bearing. If God had chosen someone other than John to write the book of revelations, I believe the verbiage would be exactly the same. We can therefore assume that every word of the text is coming directly from Jehovah God.

As Christians, it is absolutely imperative that we believe several things about the Bible. First, we must believe in the inerrancy of the scripture. This word simply means that there are no mistakes in the narratives.

Secondly we must believe that every word was divinely inspired by God himself. Here is where some liberal scholars have diverse opinions. Some believe that only the original manuscripts were divinely inspired, and that when they were translated, some human

6

error may have crept in. Knowing how vitally important God intended the Bible to be to mankind, and knowing that God has absolute total knowledge of the future, I am certain that his divine inspiration was upon the translators to the same degree that it was upon the original writers. Some ultra-liberal scholars have even put forward the theory that the original writers may have sometimes misunderstood what God was inspiring them to write. If this were the case, then the Bible becomes useless as a standard for doctrine, faith, and most importantly for instructions in the way of salvation. It then becomes readily apparent that as Christians we must believe in it's origin as divinely inspired, which is in fact, the truth!

Thirdly, the Bible is authoritative, especially the New Testament revelation of God's new covenant with man. Its edicts, commandments, and instructions are not optional, but are the standards by which God judges all mankind.

3. Blessed is he that readeth and they that hear the words of this prophesy, and keep those things which are written therein, for the time is at hand.

If we keep the words of this prophesy fresh in our hearts and minds, we will be blessed with calm and peace as we see the judgments of God unfold. Of course, during the unspeakable judgments of the tribulation we, who are born again believers, will have already been raptured out of this world, but God's judgment has been going on ever since Adam and Eve ate the forbidden fruit. As the world gets more depraved, God's judgment gets more severe. I offer Sodom and Gomorrah as an example. There will also come a time, (and I believe very soon) when tribulation for God's people will suddenly increase to the point that the unknowing may even feel that satan is getting the upper hand. (That's not a typo; I just refuse to capitalize his name). Only by knowing the scenario of the end times, and being assured that we will be victorious through Jesus Christ, can we hope to endure the "beginning of sorrows" spoken of in Mathew chapter 24. It is vital that we understand what God is about and how the conflict develops, and most importantly, how it turns out. This is extremely important to our peace of mind and soul.

4. John, to the seven churches which are in Asia; grace be unto you and peace from him which is, and which was, and which is to come; and from the seven spirits which are before his throne;

It would seem that John's salutation was exclusively for the seven churches, but when we read each letter, we find that they each end with the phrase: "Let him who hath an ear hear what the spirit saith unto the churches." The fact that the word "churches" is plural is key to understanding who the message in the letters is for. Taking the first church (Ephesus) as an example, if their letter was meant only for their congregation, the phrase would read: "Let him who hath an ear hear what the spirit saith unto the church." Therefore, combining the plurality of the word churches, and the phrase "let him who hath an ear", I can say with near certainty that the section of the book of revelations containing the letters to the seven churches is to all who read the book.

5. And from Jesus Christ who is the faithful witness, and the first begotten of the dead, and the prince of the kings of the earth. Unto him that loved us, and washed us from our sins in his own blood.

John describes Christ as Faithful Witness, First Begotten of the Dead, King of Kings, Savior, and Judge. Let us examine each of these characteristics separately.

THE FAITHFUL WITNESS Christ the son of man, God incarnate, was God's most powerful witness. Christ, the eternal glorified one is still witnessing today. It was by his testimony that I was assured of my sinful nature, and my need of a savior, and by his testimony that I discovered the remedy for both conditions. It is by his testimony that I find how I must live day by day, and by his testimony that I find how I must die. I would be most miserable, still in a lost condition, if I had all the other testimonies in the Bible without the testimony of my savior, Jesus Christ. It is also by his testimony that he becomes my mentor. Phillipians 2:5 *Let this mind*

8

be in you which was also in Christ Jesus. I Peter 2:21 *For even hereunto were ye called: because Christ also suffered for us, leaving us an example, that ye should follow his steps.*

FIRST BEGOTTEN OF THE DEAD I COR 15:20 *But now is Christ risen from the dead, and become the firstfruits of them that slept.* II COR 4:14 *Knowing that he which raised up the Lord Jesus will raise up us also by Jesus and shall present us with you.*
JOHN 6:40 *And this is the will of him that sent me, that everyone which seeeth the son, and believeth on him, may have everlasting life: and I will raise him up at the last day.*

The resurrection of Christ is proof positive of God's promise of resurrection for the saints. A major portion of the formula for salvation is stated in Romans, chapter ten, and verse nine. *That if thou shalt confess with thy mouth the Lord Jesus, and believe in thine heart that God hath raised him from the dead, thou shalt be saved.* The reason I call it a major portion rather than the whole is that this passage does not deal with repentance, which must come before one can truly confess Jesus as Lord of their life. The validity for belief in the resurrection can be summed up in two verses from the Gospel of John. First, from chapter twelve, verse thirty two: *And I, if I be lifted up from the earth, will draw all men unto me.* The second is from chapter six, verse forty: *And this is the will of him that sent me, that every one which seeth the Son, and believeth on him, may have everlasting life: and I will raise him up at the last day.* We now have the promise from Christ, through the stated will of the Father, that we, like he was, will be resurrected from the dead.

Some scoffers claim there is no proof of Jesus Christ's resurrection. The priests of the temple tried to bribe the guards into swearing that his body was stolen in the night, but the risen Christ was seen several times during a 40 day period by several of his apostles, and I COR 15:6 states that he was seen by more than 500 of the brethren. These encounters with the risen Christ took place immediately or at least shortly after his crucifixion. The advent of his crucifixion and resurrection must have drawn as much attention as the Columbine High School tragedy, or the destruction of the World Trade Center. It was most probably the main topic of conversation at every market square in every town in the area. If these encounters with the risen Christ could have been proven false it is safe to assume that the enemies of God would have done just that. They didn't because they couldn't.

PRINCE OF THE KINGS OF THE EARTH   I TIM 6:14&15   *That thou keep this commandment without spot, unrebukable, until the appearing of our Lord Jesus Christ; which in his times he shall shew who is the blessed and only potentate, the King of Kings and Lord of Lords.*   MAT 28:18 *All power is given unto me in Heaven and in earth—*
Christ's power and authority are all encompassing. As the third part of the Holy Trinity, he need merely speak and all the power of Heaven begins to move at his disposal. When he was taken before Pilate, the roman governor of Judea, accused of sedition by his countrymen, in JOHN 20:11 he declares to Pilate: *Thou couldst have no power at all against me except it were given thee from above.* Here he stood before the most powerful government of the known world, before a high authority of that government, with the power of life or death over all in his domain, and Christ seems arrogant. It could only be deemed arrogant however if it were not true! Christ was merely stating a truth. The power and authority of every world leader, past, present, and future, are on short term loan from God!

SAVIOUR what more can be said of Christ the savior?   He is the way, the truth, the life, Emanuel, God with us. We are all constantly reminded of Heaven's most precious gift; but do we consider the magnitude of his selfless act of love, or the anguish caused by the sins of all mankind? Heaven was so grieved on the day of Christ's crucifixion that the whole world went dark from the sixth until the ninth hour.
When Christ uttered the words My God, My God, why hast thou forsaken me, he took upon himself the sins of the whole world. How could one so pure and innocent endure this staggering guilt? The enormity of it was so great that only his perfect love was able to bear it. My own limited mental capacity is incapable of comprehending the utter depth of emotion that he felt in that hour.

When one considers the passion that was expended on our behalf, how can such a one possibly reject God's plan of salvation; or search for another avenue to eternity?

JUDGE   JOHN 5:22   *For the Father judgeth no man, but hath committed all judgment unto the son.*   II TIM 4:1   *I charge thee therefore before God, and the Lord Jesus Christ, who shall judge the quick and the dead at his appearing and his kingdom.*   JUDE 14 & 15   *Behold the Lord cometh with ten thousands of his saints to execute judgment upon all.*

It is hard for some Christians to visualize Christ as a fearful, righteous judge, giving no slack, and no quarter.   An intimate relationship leads us to look at him as the epitome of love, grace, and compassion, and rightly so.   This, however, is a restricted view of only one facet of the character of Christ.   While his love and compassion for mankind will never wane, there will be no room for slackness in his judgments.   His judgments will be black or white; there will be no grey areas.   Either one accepts God's plan of salvation or rejects it.   No amount of begging, pleading, excusing, or descriptions of works performed, will have any effect on the outcome.   The answer will be a straightforward yea or nay.   While Christ's love for sinner and saint alike will never change, he will be forced to say to many, *depart from me, ye that work iniquity, I never knew you.*

The word "knew" as used here must surely represent a one on one, deep personal relationship.   If it were meant to stand for just knowledge of one's existence, then it would be used incorrectly as Christ has knowledge of the existence of every individual being that has ever lived, or is living now, or will live in the future.   It is not enough for one to merely know "about" Jesus to be saved.   Salvation requires a deep, highly personal relationship.   While such a relationship is not possible physically at present, it exists spiritually in every believer from the moment of their decision to follow him.   This spiritual relationship is substantive however, in that it produces a very high degree of love, joy, peace, and the confirmation that this relationship will one day become physical as well, when Christ returns, as he has promised.   That is why believers make the claim that he "resides in us."

The absence of this intimate, spiritual relationship is what Christ refers to when he states: "I never knew you."

While we are on the subject of judgment, I feel I would be remiss if I did not point out one more verse of scripture;   HEB 9:27 *And it is appointed unto men, once to die, but after this, the judgment.*
LET THE UNDECIDED BEWARE!

6. *And hath made us kings and priests unto God and his Father; to him be glory and dominion for ever and ever.   A-men.*

While nearly all born again believers hold no earthly title of king or priest, we do stand in special privilege that is actually far more to be revered than any earthly title could possibly be worth. Throughout history, many have been chosen directly by God to serve as Kings and priests, and if their service was steadfast and subservient to his will, they were most highly regarded and rewarded for their faithfulness.   In this passage, however, I believe the Lord is reminding us not of the actual station of King or Priest, but of the similarity of our standing with God to the respect and reverence afforded to an earthly King or Priest due to their privileged position.

7. *Behold, he cometh with clouds; and every eye shall see him, and they also which pierced him; and all kindreds of the earth shall wail because of him. Even so, A-men.*

Here, John gives a prophetic warning: Behold he cometh with clouds--- I believe this prophesy heralds the second coming of Christ when he will set up his millennial kingdom.

The placement of this verse would seem to be out of place as an abundance of evidence points to his second coming at the end of the tribulation period, but I believe that John is giving mankind a solemn warning, to impress upon him the gravity of the situation, and the seriousness by which he must consider the visions and corresponding warnings that follow.   One cannot receive the full impact of the message of the book of revelations without first realizing that Jesus Christ, Son of God, will absolutely affect

12

judgment upon the whole world by his very presence when the time for such judgment is at hand.

8. I am alpha and omega, the beginning and the ending, saith the Lord, which is, and which was, and which is to come, the Almighty.

John needs no introduction to the Lord God Jehovah, John who personally walked with the only begotten son, John who forsook all that he had to follow him; no, I feel that this verse is more intended for the reader, as was verse seven, not only to impress upon him the serious nature of the visions to come, but to remind him from whom they are coming. The reader must be made aware that this is not just the imagination of an ancient, senile, human mind, but rather a direct communication from the very God of the universe.

9. I, John who also am your brother, and companion in tribulation, and in the kingdom and patience of Jesus Christ, was in the isle that is called Patmos, for the word of God, and for the testimony of Jesus Christ.
10. I was in the spirit on the Lord's day, and heard behind me a great voice, as of a trumpet,
11. saying, I am Alpha and Omega, the first and the last, and what thou seeest, write in a book, and send it unto the seven churches which are in Asia; unto Ephesus, and unto Smyrna, and unto Pergamos, and unto Thyatira, and unto Sardis, and unto Philadelphia, and unto Laodicea.

John here reveals the conditions under which he received the visions. Upon my first contact with these verses many years ago, I pictured John in my mind as a middle aged man in good health, all alone on some balmy stretch of rocky coast, with nothing to do but sit and contemplate. I suspect that many readers may have the same impression.

In all probability, none of the above is correct. When John received the visions, he was most probably working as a slave laborer in the Roman mines, and he was nearly one hundred years old. I believe neither the Roman guards nor his fellow laborers had any idea of the rapture he was experiencing, although any who looked upon him must have wondered at his countenance while he experienced the presence of God!

John is given specific instructions to deliver the visions to the churches, but I do not believe these instructions are exclusive, as the information in the visions is relevant to the entire world rather than just to those particular churches.

12. And I turned to see the voice that spake with me. And being turned, I saw seven golden candlesticks;

13. And in the midst of the seven candlesticks one like unto the Son of man, clothed with a garment down to the foot, and girt about the paps with a golden girdle.

14. His head and his hairs were white like wool, as white as snow; and his eyes were as a flame of fire;

15. And his feet like unto fine brass, as if they burned in a furnace; and his voice as the sound of many waters.

16. And he had in his right hand seven stars; and out of his mouth went a sharp twoedged sword; and his countenance was as the sun shineth in it's strength.

17. And when I saw him I fell at his feet as dead. And he laid his right hand upon me, saying unto me, fear not; I am the first and the last;

18. I am he that liveth, and was dead; and behold I am alive for evermore, Amen; and have the keys of hell and of death.

19. Write the things which thou hath seen, and the things which are, and the things which will be hereafter;

20. The mystery of the seven stars which thou sawest in my right hand, and the seven golden candlesticks. The seven stars are the angels of the seven churches; and the seven candlesticks are the seven churches.

SEVEN CANDLESTICKS AND SEVEN STARS   John sees the glorified Christ amidst the seven golden candlesticks, holding seven golden stars in his right hand. We know that the number seven in the Bible stands for completion. It is my belief that the seven candlesticks stand for Christ's complete church, and the seven stars stand for all the faithful men of God who are truly serving him as pastors.

Note that his presence is AMIDST the golden candlesticks, not above or near, praise be to God. Mathew, chapter eighteen, verse twenty: *For where two or three are gathered in my name, there am I in the midst of them.*

It is significant that he holds the pastors in his right hand. The right hand denotes power, authority, and protection.

THE SEVEN CHURCHES (chapters 2 and 3) The letters to the seven churches begin with the church at Ephesus, and continue to the churches at Smyrna, Pergamos, Thyatira, Sardis, Philadelphia, and Laodicea. It is commonly believed that John was the pastor of the church at Ephesus, and believed by many scholars that he had some oversight over the other churches, which may have been satellite churches of the church of Ephesus. All these churches were located within fifty miles of each other, on the west coast of what is now Turkey.

While there were many other churches scattered throughout the known world, why did Christ choose these particular ones so close together? Perhaps the fact that John seemed to have some influence played a part, or they may have been chosen, each for their particular failing. I tend to believe it was a combination of the two. I believe they were also chosen because their close proximity facilitated the distribution of the letters.

It would be ludicrous to assume that God inserted these letters in the book of revelations with the intent that they apply only to the named churches. While they did apply to each church specifically, there is a far more important purpose for their writing.

Each and every church that bears the name of Christian needs to honestly examine itself on an ongoing basis to see if any of these shortcomings exist, and prayerfully and humbly correct them with the utmost haste. All of these shortcomings stem from one source: A lack of faith in God's promises, and a corresponding dependency on worldly providence. God has promised to meet all our needs, and yet we tend to rely more on innovative practices than on fervent prayer.

SEVEN STAGE THEORY   There is a widely accepted theory that the seven churches represent seven stages in the development of the church as a whole, beginning with the new-born church, vibrant and on fire, and progressing through various stages of apostasy until we come to the Laodecian, or lukewarm church.   I disagree strongly with this theory.   Nearly all scholars who support this theory agree that the modern church, as a whole, is in this lukewarm stage.   On this point and on it only I tend to agree, but I see no evidence of these seven stages in the text, or in fact.   The first five stages progress from a vibrant church to a dead church, and then we come to the sixth, (Philadelphia) which seems to be a faithful church, with no criticism from the Lord, and then the seventh which is lukewarm.

To suggest that the church gradually progressed as the proponents of this theory do is also to question Christ's ability to preserve his most cherished possession.   While some churches and sometimes whole denominations have gone through temporary periods of declining purity, I am absolutely certain that Christ will always maintain a core of faithful, unspotted believers sufficient to ensure the survival of his church until the end of the church age.

While I do not subscribe to the seven stage theory, it is easy to see that an individual church could rapidly progress through the first five stages ending in a dead church, thus this theory has some merit as a tool for self examination.

As a sidebar, I would like to add that an individual Christian can just as easily go through these five stages, and often does!

Let us examine these stages, one church at a time.

CHAPTER 2

1. *Unto the angel of the church of Ephesus write; these things saith he that holdeth the seven stars in his right hand, who walketh in the midst of the seven golden candlesticks;*

2. *I know thy works, and thy labors, and thy patience, and how thou canst not bear them which are evil; and thou hast tried them which say they are apostles, and are not, and hast found them liars;*

3. *And hast borne, and hast patience, and for my name's sake hast labored, and hast not fainted.*

4. *Nevertheless I have somewhat against thee, because thou hast left thy first love.*

5. *Remember therefore from whence thou art fallen, and repent, and do the first works; or else I will come unto thee quickly, and remove thy candlestick out of his place, except thou repent.*

6. *But this thou hast; that thou hatest the deeds of the Nicolaitanes which I also hate.*

7. *He that hath an ear let him hear what the spirit saith unto the churches; to him that overcometh will I give to eat of the tree of life, which is in the midst of the paradise of God.*

The church at Ephesus was slowing down. What had begun with great zeal as a labor of love had become commonplace. This church had become apathetic. (Lacking emotion). Church attendance only out of a sense of duty is lacking in zeal. A true born again believer, filled with the spirit, will place church attendance above all other pursuits and their church attendance will definitely show it. Their conduct during worship will demonstrate joy and exuberance rather than complacency. It will be their earnest desire to be present whenever the doors are open.

8. *And unto the angel of the church in Smyrna write; these things sayeth the first, and the last, which was dead and is alive;*

9. I know thy works, and tribulation, and poverty (but thou art rich) and I know the blasphemy of them which say they are Jews, and are not, but are the synagogue of satan.

10. Fear none of those things that thou shalt suffer: behold the devil shall cast some of you into prison, that ye may be tried; and ye shall have tribulation ten days: be thou faithful unto death, and I will give thee a crown of life.

11. He that hath an ear, let him hear what the spirit saith unto the churches; he that overcometh shall not be hurt of the second death.

This apathy of Ephesus could easily lead to the problem with the church at Smyrna. It would seem from the text that they suffered some financial problems, and were fearful of some persecution that was ongoing, or at least heading their way. A lack of faith in God's providence and protection had caused them to feel threatened.

12. And to the angel of the church in Pergamos write; these things saith he which hath the sharp sword with two edges;

13. I know thy works, and where thou dwellest, even where satan's seat is; and thou holdest fast my name, and hast not denied my faith, even in those days wherein Antipas was my faithful martyr, who was slain among you, where satan dwelleth.

14. But I have a few things against thee, because thou hast there them that hold to the doctrine of Balaam, who taught Balac to cast a stumbling block before the children of Israel, to eat things sacrificed unto idols, and to commit fornication.

15. So hast thou also them which hold the doctrine of the Nicolitanes which thing I hate.

16. Repent; or else I will come unto thee quickly, and will fight against them with the sword of my mouth.

17. He that hath an ear, let him hear what the spirit saith unto the churches; to him that overcometh will I give to eat of the hidden manna, and will give him a white stone, and in the stone a new name written, which no man knoweth save him who receiveth it.

Feeling threatened (as did Smyrna), could easily lead to the sin of the church of Pergamos. Perhaps it was an effort to fit in to the community, thus appeasing the source of the persecution, or it was done in an effort to expand their membership in order to have strength in numbers, perhaps it was a little of both, but they began to tolerate false doctrines. God specifically mentions two separate doctrines that they have allowed in their midst that were contrary to his word. Whether they had realized it or not, they had compromised with the devil.

18. And unto the angel of the church in Thyatira write; These things saith the Son of God, who hath his eyes like unto a flame of fire, and his feet are like fine brass;

19. I know thy works, and charity, and service, and faith, and thy patience; and thy works; and the last to be more than the first.

20. Not withstanding I have a few things against thee, because thou sufferest that woman Jezebel, which calleth herself a prophetess, to teach and to seduce my servants to commit fornication, and to eat things sacrificed unto idols.

21. And I gave her space to repent of her fornication, and she repented not.

22. Behold, I will cast her into a bed, and them that commit adultery with her into great tribulation, except they repent of their deeds.

23. And I will kill her children with death, and all the churches shall know that I am he which searcheth the reins and hearts; and I will give unto every one of you according to your works,

24. But unto you I say, and unto the rest in Thyatira, as many as have not this doctrine, and which have not known the depths of satan, as they speak; I will put upon you none other burden.

25. But that which ye have already hold fast till I come.

26. And he that overcometh, and keepeth my works unto the end, to him will I give power over the nations;

27. And he shall rule them with a rod of iron; as the vessels of a potter shall they be broken to shivers: even as I received of my father.

28. And I will give him the morning star.

29. He that hath an ear, let him hear what the Spirit saith unto the churches.

Once a church begins to tolerate false doctrines, this could easily lead to the sin of the church of Thyatira. False prophets and teachers were openly allowed to practice in their midst. I believe that they were not only allowed to practice openly, but also that they were known to be false by the church leadership, who knew what needed to be done, but were afraid to do it. They were more interested in popularity than in purity.

CHAPTER 3

1. And unto the angel of the church in Sardis write; These things saith he that hath the seven spirits of God, and the seven stars; I know thy works, that thou hast a name, that thou livest, and art dead.

2. Be watchful, and strengthen the things which remain, that are ready to die: for I have not found thy works perfect before God.

3. Remember therefore how thou hast received and heard, and hold fast, and repent. If therefore thou shalt not watch, I shall come on thee as a thief, and thou shalt not know what hour I will come upon thee.

4. Thou hast a few names even in Sardis which have not defiled their garments; and they shall walk with me in white: for they are worthy.

5. He that overcometh the same shall be clothed in white raiment; and I will not blot out his name out of the book of life, but I will confess his name before my Father, and before his angels.

6. He that hath an ear, let him hear what the Spirit saith unto the churches.

The next step is tragic. The church at Sardis was dead. They still held meetings, conducted programs, nominated committees, but the spirit had left. We know that their doors were still open because their letter was to be delivered to them, and also in the letter Christ instructs the faithful few to hang on and build on what remains, but for all practical purposes, this church is useless to him. The devil had succeeded in what he does best. He will entice a church, or a believer, to commit one little tiny infraction, just this once; it won't do any harm. And then the next time he convinces us to go just a little farther ETC. ETC. We can see here the tragic end of this progression.

7. And to the angel of the church in Philadelphia write; These things saith he that is holy, he that is true, he that hath the key of David, he that openeth and no man shutteth; and shutteth, and no man openeth;

8. I know thy works: behold I have set before thee an open door, and no man can shut it: for thou hast a little strength, and hast kept my word, and hast not denied my name.

9. Behold I will make them of the synagogue of satan, which say they are Jews, and are not, but do lie; behold, I will make them to come and worship before thy feet, and to know that I have loved thee.

10. Because thou hast kept the word of my patience, I will also keep thee from the hour of temptation, which shall come upon all the world, to try them that dwell upon the earth.

11. Behold, I come quickly: hold that fast which thou hast, that no man take thy crown.

12. Him that overcometh will I make a pillar in the temple of my God, and he shall go no more out: and I shall write upon him the name of my God, and the name of the city of my God, which is New Jerusalem, which cometh down out of Heaven from my God: and I will write upon him my new name.

13. He that hath an ear let him hear what the Spirit saith unto the churches.

Now we come to the church at Philadelphia. We now depart from the gradual downhill slide of the first five churches, which is one of the main reasons that I do not accept the seven stages theory. This church is a faithful church. Christ has no chastisement for this church as he has for the other six. It is my belief that this demonstrates that even in the midst of widespread apostasy, a church can still maintain it's purity as long as it holds to the faith and sound biblical doctrine, without compromise.

14. And unto the angel of the church of the Laodiceans write; These things saith the Amen, the faithful and true witness, the beginning of the creation of God;

15. I know thy works that thou art neither cold nor hot: I would thou wert cold or hot.

16. So then, because thou art lukewarm, and neither cold nor hot, I will spue thee out of my mouth.

17. Because thou sayest, I am rich, and increased with goods, and have need of nothing: and knowest not that thou art wretched, and miserable, and poor, and blind, and naked:

18. I counsel thee to buy of me gold tried in the fire, that thou mayest be rich; and with raiment that thou mayest be clothed, and that the shame of thy nakedness do not appear; and anoint thine eyes with eye salve that thou mayest see.

19. As many as I love, I rebuke and chasten: be zealous therefore and repent.

20. Behold, I stand at the door and knock: if any man hear my voice, and open the door, I will come in to him, and sup with him, and he with me.

21. To him that overcometh will I grant to sit with me in my throne, even as I also overcame, and am sit down with my Father in his throne.

22. He that hath an ear let him hear what the Spirit saith unto the churches.

I believe that the Laodicean church is a product of an attitude that is prevalent today in all walks of life; the idea of doing just enough to get by. I would consider this church to be representative of the modern church today. Of course, He's talking about somebody else's' church, not mine, right? (Think about it). The big problem here is that the church has decided what is just enough to get by, and expects God to be satisfied with their choice, when, in reality, their choice comes far short of what God expects. They think they are doing alright but Christ says I will spew thee out of my mouth. Many churches today, as well as many individual Christians rate themselves by a process I call "comparison righteousness". They measure their progress against the church next door, or the man across the street when they should be comparing themselves to what the word of God says they should be. This practice of comparison righteousness invariably leads to a false sense of well-doing, and results in a church or a believer that is of little or no use to the Lord.

At the close of each letter Christ makes the same statement: He that hath an ear, let him hear what the spirit saith unto the churches. Note that the rest of the text is singular, specific to the intended church, but this ending is plural, indicating that the letter is to be shared. Shared with whom? With anyone that hath an ear.

Christ also lists one or more rewards in each letter. These rewards can be grouped together, and all apply to him who overcometh.

To him that overcometh will I give to eat of the tree of life.

Be thou faithful unto death and I will give thee a crown of life.

He that overcometh shall not be hurt of the second death.

To him that overcometh will I give to eat of the hidden manna, and will give him a white stone, and in the stone a new name written, which no man knoweth save he that receiveth it.

And he that overcometh, and keepeth my works unto the end, to him will I give power over the nations---and I will give him the morning star.

He that overcometh the same shall be clothed in white raiment; and I will not blot his name out of the book of life, and I will confess his name before my Father and before his angels.

Him that overcometh will I make a pillar in the temple of my God, and he shall go no more out: and I will write upon him the name of my God and the name of the city of my God, which is new Jerusalem which cometh down out of Heaven from my God; and I will write upon him my new name.

To him that overcometh will I grant to sit with me on my throne, even as I also overcame, and am set down with my Father on his throne.

CHAPTER 4

Up to this point, the introduction and the seven letters are fairly easy to understand. In chapter 4, we see a major change in that John sees visions that are complex, and their meaning is somewhat elusive. God, in his infinite wisdom, knows that some of the knowledge of the future of mankind cannot be revealed to man all at once. God knows that it would be detrimental to man's well being. As an example, would you like to know the exact date and hour that you are going to die? Would you like for your obituary to be a part of your birth certificate? Any reasonable person would say "of course not".

When we read the book of revelations we are left with a partial knowledge that something specific is going to happen, but we don't know all the details. That is precisely what God wants us to see at this time.

JOHN'S FIRST VISION

1. After this I looked, and behold, a door was opened in Heaven: and the first voice I heard was as of a trumpet talking with me; which said, come up hither, and I will shew thee things which must be hereafter.
2. And immediately I was in the spirit: and, behold, a throne was set in Heaven, and one sat on the throne.
3, And he that sat was to look upon like a jasper and a sardine stone: and there was a rainbow round about the throne, in sight like unto an emerald.

John is transported to Heaven, probably in the spirit, possibly in both body and spirit, and he hears the voice of Christ. His description of the things he saw is so wonderful, one can only anxiously anticipate with great desire their own viewing. Christ says: "come hither and I will shew thee things which must be hereafter".

Of course the use of the word hereafter leaves no doubt that the things he is about to see are a vision of future events. There are widely varied interpretations of the "time-line" of the book of revelations. Some consider portions of the book to be historical and the rest to be prophetic in varying mixes, while others consider it to be both historical and prophetic at the same time. I submit that based on the statement of Christ himself, all the visions from this point, can only describe the period beginning with the first day of the tribulation (with some few exceptions) and ending with the end of time.

The fact that he used the word "must" is interesting terminology. You see, the judgments of God "must" be, as the rebellion of satan and the depravity of man demand it. God is not forcing his judgment on a hapless world; a sinful world has forced God to take drastic measures. If God had a less severe option, he would, by his compassionate nature, certainly take it.

4. And round about the throne were four and twenty seats: and upon the seats I saw four and twenty elders sitting, clothed in white raiment; and they had on their heads crowns of gold.

THE TWENTY FOUR ELDERS

John sees twenty four elders. Some scholars believe they represent the twelve tribes of Israel, but I would ask them: Why two from each tribe? I prefer to believe that they represent the tribes of Israel, and the raptured gentile church.

JOHN 10:16 reads in part: *And other sheep I have, which are not of this fold: them also I must bring---*

I believe that twelve represent the nation of Israel, and twelve represent the gentile church, showing that while the Israelites are God's chosen people throughout all history on the earth; God has no partiality in Heaven for either group.

5. And out of the throne proceeded lightnings and thunderings and voices: and there were seven lamps of fire burning before the throne, which are the seven spirits of God.

THE LIGHTNINGS, THUNDERINGS, AND VOICES

We read that John saw lightning, and heard thunderings and voices. Most of us picture Heaven as a quiet, serene, idyllic place. I suppose that is one of the reasons for the vow of silence taken by some monastic orders. Perhaps they are trying to duplicate, as far as possible, the conditions of Heaven, as they picture it. While Heaven is an absolutely perfect place, I believe that it is much more dynamic than most people visualize, with myriads of events occurring constantly. I don't believe that God just sits and waits. I submit the vision of Jacob's ladder, where Jacob saw a steady stream of angels both ascending, and descending to accomplish the will of God. While many of us have never physically seen an angel, (I submit that many have without knowing it), we all agree that they exist and are constantly ministering at God's command. I believe that the thunder and lightning and voices are representative of the constant activity that takes place in Heaven and on earth under the divine control of Jehovah God. At the time that this vision represents, the judgments of God are about to begin, and this entails a tremendous amount of preparation.

John saw seven lamps of fire and identifies them as the seven spirits of God. This is a puzzling vision. How can an inanimate object such as a lamp burning with fire be called a spirit? First off, I would remind the reader that this is not an explanation conjured up by John, but something he was divinely inspired to write by the spirit of God.

Throughout the Bible, after the fall of Adam and Eve, whenever God came into the presence of any person or group of persons to any degree, he was always accompanied and partially shielded by fire. The burning bush seen by Moses, The pillar of fire by night seen by the Israelites in the desert, and the smoke and fire on Mount Sinai seen by Moses and the people are all instances of this. In every case this fire was twofold. It denoted the presence of God without actually revealing his person; and it was a protective buffer zone between man and God. For mortal man to look clearly upon God in his entire splendor would result in instant death.

It is therefore my assumption that these seven lamps were a mask to prevent John from looking directly upon God while still recognizing his presence.   I believe that the reason God identified them to John as the seven spirits of God is to represent the completeness and the complexity of God.   As previously stated the number seven in Bible numerology stands for completeness and the book of revelations is saturated with sevens as no other book of the Bible.   In the next chapter, we will find out more about the seven spirits of God.

6. And before the throne there was a sea of glass like unto crystal: and in the midst the throne, and round about the throne, were four beasts full of eyes before and behind.
7. And the first beast was like a lion, and the second beast like a calf, and the third beast had a face as a man, and the fourth beast was like a flying eagle.
8. And the four beasts had each of them six wings about him; and they were full of eyes within: and they rest not day and night, saying Holy, holy, holy, Lord God Almighty, which was, and is, and is to come.

THE FOUR BEASTS
    Whenever one uses the word beast, A picture automatically materializes of something grotesque.   I cannot picture anything in Heaven being ugly.   In this case, I believe the term is used to describe four special angels.   Many futile attempts have been made to identify these creatures but I submit that the Bible tells us the following:

1. They are Heavenly creatures.
2. They were created by God, for God.
3. They praise God day and night.

    Anything further would be pure speculation.   There are, however, some clues to their possible identity in Isaiah, chapter 6, and Ezekiel, chapter 10. Each of these chapters describe four creatures remarkably similar in appearance to the ones John saw. In all three cases, they seem to have a special purpose in connection with the throne of God. These creatures in the book of Isaiah, chapter 6, are identified as Seraphim. In the book of Isaiah, one of the four Seraphim takes a fiery coal from the altar of God to purify the prophets lips. In the book of Ezekiel, chapter 10, one of the four creatures, here identified as Cherubim, takes a handful of coals from the altar and hands them to God's avenger. While the other angels are going to and fro, doing God's bidding, it would seem that these four creatures are assigned a special purpose in conjunction with the Heavenly throne, which is their constant abode.

9. And when those beasts give glory and honor and thanks to him that sat on the throne, who liveth for ever and ever,
10. The four and twenty elders fall down before him that sat on the throne, and worship him that liveth for ever and ever, and cast their crowns before the throne saying,
11. Thou art worthy, O Lord, to receive glory and honor and power: for thou hast created all things, and for thy pleasure they are and were created.

Here we see the typical worship that occurs in Heaven on a continuing basis. Note the awe and reverence that are accorded to the Lord, and contrast this with our typical worship service of today. This awe and reverence was present in the early patriarchs, but modern man has managed to humanize God to the degree that allows man to now consider God to be only a little higher than man. We treat our obligation to honor and revere him as optional, dependent upon his treatment of us! We afford higher esteem to the elders of our family than we do the God of the universe.

CHAPTER 5

1. *And I saw in the right hand of him that sat on the throne a book written within and on the backside, sealed with seven seals.*
2. *And I saw a strong angel proclaiming with a loud voice, who is worthy to open the book, and loose the seven seals thereof?*
3. *And no man in Heaven, nor in earth, neither under the earth, was able to open the book, neither to look thereon.*
4. *And I wept much, because no man was found worthy to open and to read the book, neither to look thereon.*
5. *And one of the elders saith unto me, weep not: behold, the lion of the tribe of Judah, the root of David, hath prevailed to open the book, and to loose the seven seals thereof.*
6. *And I beheld and, lo, in the midst of the throne and of the four beasts, and in the midst of the elders, stood a Lamb as it had been slain, having seven horns and seven eyes, which are the seven spirits of God sent forth into all the earth.*
7. *And he came and took the book out of the right hand of him that sat on the throne.*
8. *And when he had taken the book, the four beast and the four and twenty elders fell down before the Lamb, having every one of them harps, and golden vials full of odors, which are the prayers of the saints.*
9. *And they sung a new song, saying, thou art worthy to take the book and to open the seals thereof: for thou wast slain, and hast redeemed us to God by thy blood out of every kindred, and tongue, and people, and nation;*
10. *And hast made us unto our God kings and priests: and we shall reign on the earth.*

THE SEVEN SEALS

The Lamb "prevailed" to open the book: also in verse 6, John saw "A Lamb that was slain". These words point to the fact that this event happens after his victory on the cross. This negates the theory that some have put forward that the four horses represent stages in the development of mankind from the book of Genesis until the end of the world. A much more believable explanation is that they represent future events that will take place during the reign of the antichrist; during the tribulation period. One of the reasons that I believe this is that during the period of the fourth horse, the narrative states that a fourth part of the world's population was slain. While wholesale slaughter has been practiced all too often by mankind throughout history, there has never been a period where we even came close to a fourth part of the population, therefore this must be a portrayal of the future.

Nearly all Bible scholars agree that the tribulation period will last for seven years. They also agree for the most part, that for the first three and one half years, the antichrist will rule as a benevolent benefactor, thus endearing himself to the masses, especially to the nation of Israel. Once he has established his position, and consolidated his power, he will do a complete reversal and become a tyrant. It is my belief that nearly all of this seven year period is represented by the seven seals. I believe there will be a very short period at the very end of the seven years when God's judgment will take place.

Note in verse six, that the Lamb, which clearly represents the crucified, risen Christ, is seen by John as having seven horns and seven eyes which are the seven spirits of God.
These seven spirits are further identified in the book of Isaiah, 11:2 in speaking of the Lord Jesus who is yet to come: *And the spirit of (1)* **the Lord** *shall rest upon him, the spirit of (2)***wisdom** *and (3)***understanding***, the spirit of (4)***counsel** *and (5)***might***, the spirit of (6)***knowledge** *and the (7)***fear of the Lord***.

In chapter 5, John sees a vision of the scroll with seven seals, in the hand of God. The events that John witness clearly depict that the age of God's judgment has come. This vision unmistakably reveals that all judgment has been placed in the hands of Christ, the Lamb of God.

11. And I beheld, and I heard the voice of many angels round about the throne and the beasts and the elders: and the number of them was ten thousand times ten thousand, and thousands of thousands;

12. Saying with a loud voice worthy is the Lamb that was slain to receive power, and riches, and wisdom, and strength, and honor, and glory, and blessing.

13. And every creature which is in Heaven, and on the earth, and under the earth, and such as are in the sea, and all that are in them, heard I saying, blessing, and honor, and glory, and power, be unto him that sitteth upon the throne, and unto the Lamb for ever and ever.

14. And the four beasts said A-men.   And the four and twenty elders fell down and worshipped him that liveth for ever and ever.

Once again we see the awe and reverence that are present in true worship.   There is great rejoicing as though all Heaven was patiently awaiting this event.   Note in verse 11 the number of worshipers: ten thousand times ten thousand and thousands of thousands.   Many scholars have tried to decipher this number, but I will only say that the words "great multitude" do not even suffice. Those that think Heaven will be sparsely populated are in for a great surprise!

CHAPTER 6

1. *And I saw when the Lamb opened one of the seals, and I heard as it were the noise of thunder, one of the four beasts saying, come and see.*
2. *And I saw, and behold: a white horse, and he that sat on him had a bow; and a crown was given unto him: and he went forth conquering and to conquer.*

THE WHITE HORSE (FIRST SEAL)

Various attempts have been made to identify the rider of the white horse as a specific being, to wit: Christ, or even the antichrist. If we look at all four horses, we see that the emphasis is on the horses rather than the riders. If one must put a label on the rider of the white horse, I would call him "world governments" rather than one specific individual.

At various points in history, great and powerful leaders of mankind have made gargantuan attempts to bring about world peace, with varying degrees of temporary success. In the beginning of the reign of the antichrist, there will be a period when the whole world will feel a false sense of security. Intellectual man will be convinced that he has finally risen above his carnal nature and become a noble being, worthy of recognition in the universe. This intellectual pride will replace dependency on God; God will become passé in the mind of modern man. Phrases like "new world order" are already being bandied about today, and the time is near for the emergence of the antichrist and his one world government based on the false premise that mankind can secure his own peace.

JEREMIAH 13:10 reads in part: *Because, even because they have seduced my people, saying peace; and there is no peace---* This false peace signified by the vision of the white horse will be man made, and will not last. Note the terminology used in 6:2: he went forth conquering and to conquer. It does not merely say that he conquered.   The use of the phrase "to conquer" means to me that total conquest is not completely achieved.   While mankind has a desire to conquer his base nature, he has only had limited temporary successes.   Through his own efforts, without the Lordship of Christ, totality is unattainable.

3. And when he had opened the second seal, I heard the second beast say, come and see.
4. And there went out another horse that was red: and power was given to him that sat thereon to take peace from the earth, and that they should kill one another: and there was given unto him a great sword.

THE RED HORSE (SECOND SEAL)

The red horse represents conflict.   While the antichrist will secure a short period of peace, there will still be undercurrents of unrest, evolving eventually into open rebellion.   Note in verse four, that peace will be taken from the earth, and they will kill one another.   A majority of the world today believes there is a God, but many do not believe the gospel message.   These see Christian moral values as an unnecessary restriction on their intellectual lifestyle, and therefore resent the propagation of Christianity.   They will gladly follow the antichrist in great numbers, zealously participating in the persecution of all who hold to Judeo-Christian principles.   This animosity toward true believers is present and growing today at an alarming rate.

Many believers during this period will be faced with an ominous choice: denounce their beliefs or face death!

In this conflict, represented by the red horse, the antichrist will prevail and vanquish all resistance.

5. And when he had opened the third seal, I heard the third beast say, come and see.   And I beheld, and lo, a black horse; and he that sat on him had a pair of balances in his hand.
6. And I heard a voice in the midst of the four beasts say, a measure of wheat for a penny, and three measures of barley for a penny; and see thou hurt not the oil and the wine.

THE BLACK HORSE (THIRD SEAL)

The black horse represents famine. I believe this famine will be twofold. It is easy to see where the constant conflict represented by the red horse would bring about physical famine, but there will be an even more serious spiritual famine, the likes of which mankind has never seen before. Sometime during the reign of the antichrist, the one world church will be established. My estimation is that it will be done during the early part of his reign. Even today there are some who would like to see a unified world church, and it will only take someone with worldwide authority to make it so. At first, I expect this one world church to be optional, but as it gains support through the favor of the antichrist, it will become mandatory and all other churches will be banned and criminalized. The head of this church will be none other than the antichrist himself, through his false prophet.

The physical famine of this period will be vast and hard felt, but there will be especially hard times for all who will not bow to the antichrist and his forces. It is during this period that the mark of the beast will come into play, and the very necessities of life will be deliberately withheld from all who will not worship the antichrist. Those who refuse the mark will not be able to buy, sell, receive medical needs, have access to transportation, or take part in any political process. It will be a time of merciless, despotic rule by the antichrist. He will not only require absolute obedience, but will demand that he be worshipped as god.

7. And when he had opened the fourth seal, I heard the voice of the fourth beast say, come and see.
8. And I looked, and behold a pale horse: and his name that sat on him was death, and hell followed with him. And power was given unto them over the fourth part of the earth, to kill with sword, and with hunger, and with death, and with the beasts of the earth.

THE PALE HORSE (FOURTH SEAL)

The tyrannical rule of the antichrist has finally come to full fruition. His seven year rule has clearly demonstrated man's inability to effect peace and harmony in a godless society. Society is in shambles, and one fourth of the world's population dies prematurely, and violently, through various causes. What had begun as a quest for world peace has resulted in total anarchy. The antichrist and his forces are incapable of affecting a remedy. Instead of the hoped for Utopia, utter despair has become the order of the day.

9. And when he had opened the fifth seal, I saw under the altar the souls of them that were slain for the word of God, and for the testimony which they held·

10. And they cried with a loud voice, saying, how long, o Lord, holy and true, dost thou not judge and avenge our blood on them that dwell on the earth?

11. and white robes were given unto every one of them; and it was said unto them, that they should rest yet for a little season, until their fellow servants also and their brethren, that should be killed as they were, should be fulfilled.

THE FIFTH SEAL

The fifth seal is opened and we see the Christian martyrs, before the throne of God, asking him when he will avenge their death. It would seem from the text that they were impatient, much like most people today. When we see things that don't look right, things that we don't understand, we plead with God to do something right now. We remind him of what is happening as if he may have been too busy to notice. God is all seeing, all knowing, all powerful, there is nothing that misses his attention. We can be totally secure in the knowledge that when the time is right, God will act decisively, with divine wisdom.

I believe that these martyrs are from the tribulation period, as they seem to be new arrivals. This is suggested by the fact that they are issued white robes in verse eleven; and that there were still others yet to be slain under the same conditions.

12. And I beheld when he had opened the sixth seal, and, lo, there was a great earthquake; and the sun became black as sackcloth of hair, and the moon became as blood;

13. And the stars of Heaven fell upon the earth, even as a fig tree casteth her untimely figs, when she is shaken of a mighty wind.

14. And the heaven departed as a scroll when it is rolled together; and every mountain and island were moved out of their places.

15. And the kings of the earth, and the great men, and the rich men, and the chief captains, and the mighty men, and every bondman, and every free man, hid themselves in the dens and in the rocks of the mountains;

16. And said to the mountains and rocks, fall on us, and hide us from the face of him that sittith on the throne, and from the wrath of the Lamb:

17. For the great day of his wrath is come; and who shall be able to stand?

THE SIXTH SEAL

The sixth seal signals a distinct departure from the status quo. Up until this point, satan, the antichrist, and secular mankind, have been left to their own devices with no divine intervention, except for God's witnesses. The fact that God is now taking control is indicative that the sixth seal is opened near the end of the tribulation period. Note that in difference to the judgments to come, which will bring great physical harm upon mankind, these events of the sixth seal bring little or no harm to living creatures, including mankind, but are designed to get the attention of all on earth. God gives man opportunity after opportunity to change his ways. While his patience is great, it is not limitless. God knows when the last soul will repent, and the time for judgment is at hand.

I find mankind's response in verses sixteen and seventeen to be pretty much predictable in that he seems to know that God himself is causing these terrible events to happen, but he still will not repent and accept God's offer of grace.

We now come to an interlude between the sixth and seventh seals in which John is shown a vision that does not fit in the timeline of events. The first through sixth seals cover nearly all of the tribulation period, and this vision covers two groups that were active during the tribulation, probably from the beginning.

CHAPTER 7

TWO GROUPS OF SAINTS

1. And after these things I saw four angels standing on the four corners of the earth, holding the four winds of the earth, that the wind should not blow on the earth, nor on the sea, nor on any tree.
2. And I saw another angel ascending from the east, having the seal of the living God: and he cried with a loud voice to the four angels, to whom it was given to hurt the earth and the sea,
3. Saying, hurt not the earth, neither the sea, nor the trees, till we have sealed the servants of our God in their foreheads.
4. And I heard the number of them which were sealed: and there were sealed an hundred and forty four thousand of all the tribes of the children of Israel.
5. Of the tribe of Judah were sealed twelve thousand. Of the tribe of Ruben were sealed twelve thousand. Of the tribe of Gad were sealed twelve thousand.
6. Of the tribe of Aser were sealed twelve thousand. Of the tribe of Nepthalim were sealed twelve thousand. Of the tribe of Manasses were sealed twelve thousand.
7. Of the tribe of Simeon were sealed twelve thousand. Of the tribe of Levi were sealed twelve thousand. Of the tribe of Issachar were sealed twelve thousand.
8. Of the tribe of Zabulon were sealed twelve thousand. Of the tribe of Joseph were sealed twelve thousand. Of the tribe of Benjamin were sealed twelve thousand.

John witnesses the sealing of 144,000 Jews with a mark on their forehead. This sealing takes place on earth, probably at or at least near the beginning of the tribulation. The exact timing cannot be accurately determined but there are some clues. In verse 3 we read: saying hurt not the earth, neither the sea, nor the trees, till we have sealed the servants of our God in their forehead. By this, we can be almost certain that the sealing takes place at least prior to the sixth seal. In chapter 14 of the book of revelation, we see the 144,000 mentioned again, and it would seem from the text that they are performing some ministry for Christ on the earth during the tribulation, so the sealing would most probably be done at or near the beginning of the tribulation.

The 144,000 are identified as being from specific tribes of Israel. I can perceive no other reason for so accurate identification than that this description is to be taken literally.

There is somewhat of a puzzle in the list of tribes. There have been various solutions to this puzzle offered, but none substantiated to my knowledge.

In the book of Joshua, when the Israelites were dividing their inheritance in the land of Caanan, at the direction of God, there were actually fourteen tribes participating. There were the twelve natural sons of Jacob, and he had adopted his two grandchildren, Ephraim and Mannaseh, sons of Joseph, who also each received an inheritance.

Now here is the puzzle. Of these fourteen tribes, only twelve are listed in the 144,000. One grandson, Ephraim, and one natural son, Dan, are left out. As I said before, many have speculated on the reason for this omission, but no reason can be found in scripture. I can only assume that God selected them at his pleasure. He need not explain his decisions, nor should anyone ever claim private knowledge of his motives. It is enough for us to know that he will do it. If it were necessary for us to know his reasons, he would provide them.

9. After this I beheld, and, lo, a great multitude, which no man could number, of all nations, and, kindreds, and people, and tongues, stood before the throne, and before the Lamb, clothed with white robes and, palms in their hands;
10. And cried with a loud voice, saying, salvation to our God which sitteth upon the throne, and unto the Lamb.

11. And all the angels stood round about the throne, and about the elders and the four beasts, and fell before the throne on their faces, and worshipped God.

12. Saying A-men: Blessing, and glory, and wisdom, and thanksgiving, and honor, and power, and might, be unto God for ever and ever, A-men.

13. And one of the elders answered saying unto me, What are these which are arrayed in white robes? And whence came they?

14. And I said unto him, sir, thou knowest. And he said unto me, these are they which came out of great tribulation, and have washed their robes, and made them white in the blood of the Lamb.

15. Therefore are they before the throne of God, and serve him day and night in his temple: and he that sitteth on the throne shall dwell among them.

16. They shall hunger no more, neither thirst any more; neither shall the sun light on them, nor any heat.

17. For the Lamb which is in the midst of the throne shall feed them, and shall lead them unto living fountains of waters: and God shall wipe away all tears from their eyes.

John sees a second group which no man could number, of all nations, and kindreds, and peoples, and tongues. These are identified by one of the elders as they which came out of great tribulation, and have washed their robes, and made them white in the blood of the Lamb. There is some controversy as to whether John sees this group in Heaven, or on earth, the scripture gives no clue, but the important thing to remember is that they exist. It is my belief that this group is the raptured church, and they are in heaven. Only during the age of grace, (the church age), would they have had the opportunity to wash their robes in the blood of the Lamb.

Here we come to a concept that many readers of the book of revelations fail to grasp. There is often more than one interpretation of a particular vision. We, in this day and time, consider the book to be relevant to OUR future, and rightly so, but consider this: The book of revelations was circulated among Christiandom from about 95 A.D. until the present. It held future prophesy for those early readers as well.   What is now history to us was still future in their time.

There have been periods in the past when the true believers were persecuted to a degree and intensity resembling that of the tribulation period.   Some Roman emperors embraced the spread of Christianity, while others persecuted Christians mercilessly.   In its early stages, the church had every reason to doubt its very survival, but thank God for those who persevered, and it is my belief that the book of revelations was a great source of strength and faith to those early believers.

Before we continue, I would like to say something to my Catholic brothers and sisters.   Some of you may take offense at what I am about to write, but there is no need to do so.   The actions and policies I am about to describe are not those of the current Catholic church.   They represent only a brief period in its history, and the church recognized and corrected the excesses of that period.   I am merely stating these facts to show how important the book of revelations was to those early Christians.

One case in point was the reformation period.   In the late fourteen hundreds, the church had become so involved in politics, and the politicians had become so involved in the church, that the Catholic Church had for all practical purposes become one world church, decreed by the governments of men.   The doctrine of salvation by grace through the blood of the Lamb, as taught by Christ and the apostles, had been replaced by a report card system, and anyone who disagreed with the teachings of the church was punished as a heretic.

Many who held to the teachings of Christ were tortured and martyred in horrible ways for their beliefs.   One notable figure was Joan of Arc who was burned as a witch.

The church had its own private religious police force known as the "Inquisition".

This force was to seek out heretics, and punish them for their sins.   The examination was almost always a form of torture that ended in death.   If the accused broke during the torture and confessed, his punishment was death.   If he did not break, the examination was usually continued until he died.   An accusation of heresy became quite popular as a very efficient means to eliminate political or social rivals. The inquisition operated their own prisons and torture chambers which were usually more gruesome than the secular penal institutions of the times.

During this period, men like Martin Luther began to break away from the misguided traditions of the church. It was during this period that the major denominations of the protestant church were formed, thus the name reformation period.

The spiritual situation during the reformation period was much the same as it will be during the reign of the antichrist. There was one world church, based on the doctrines of men, and true believers were prosecuted. Now picture yourself as a believer during this time. As you read of this great multitude that had come out of great tribulation by the power of God, would this not give you the strength and courage to endure?

While I do not suggest that this vision should represent to us today what it did to those who were martyred during the reformation period, it must have represented just that to the believer in Martin Luther's day. This vision became a source of hope to those believers, just as it does to us today.

One might think that God was being deceitful to those early believers, but if you consider the vision to be both symbolic and literal, there is nothing deceitful about it having one meaning to those believers, and a different meaning to us today. God's purpose in supplying this vision to his believers is to give them hope and strength to endure in times of great hardship, and it does that wonderfully in each case.

0CHAPTER 8

1. And when he had opened the seventh seal, there was silence in Heaven about the space of half an hour.

2. And I saw the seven angels which stood before God; and to them were given seven trumpets.

THE SEVENTH SEAL

There was silence in Heaven about the space of half an hour. God's judgment upon evil man is about to unfold, and all Heaven stands in silent awe at the enormity of what is about to happen.

While returning from a Wednesday night Bible study where we were discussing how awesome God's judgment will be, my twelve year old grandson said: "Grandpa, God tells us we have to turn the other cheek. Why doesn't he do the same thing?" After considerable thought, I answered his question with another question: "What would happen if he did?" To which he replied: "We would probably destroy ourselves." "Right, so in order to save the good part of his creation, he has to destroy the bad part" was my reply.

Later, while going over our conversation, I realized that in reality, God did turn the other cheek by sacrificing his only begotten son in our behalf. God takes absolutely no pleasure in the destruction of any part of his creation.

II PETER 3:9 *The Lord is not slack concerning his promise, as some men count slackness; but is long suffering to us-ward, not willing that any should perish, but that all should come to repentance.*

JOHN 3:16 *For God so loved the world that he sent his only begotten son, that whosoever believeth in him should not perish, but have everlasting life.*

That sure seems like turning the other cheek to me!

3. *And another angel came and stood at the altar, having a golden censer; and there was given to him much incense, that he should offer it with the prayers of all saints upon the golden altar which was before the throne.*
4. *And the smoke of the incense which came with the prayers of the saints, ascended up before God out of the angel's hand.*
5. *And the angel took the censer, and filled it with fire of the altar, and cast it into the earth: and there were voices, and thunderings, and lightnings, and an earthquake.*

THE ANGEL WITH THE GOLDEN CENSER

The angel with the golden censer is thought by some scholars to be Christ himself, due to the fact that the prayers of the saints are to be offered through him only, but I disagree for three reasons.

First, nowhere in any of his other writings does John identify Christ as an angel.

I have heard more than one preacher say that when the Bible speaks of THE angel of God, rather than AN angel of God that this speaks of Christ. I can prove them wrong with one verse of scripture. Mathew chapter 28, verse 2 reads: *And behold there was a great earthquake: for THE angel of the Lord descended from Heaven, and came and rolled back the stone from the door, and sat upon it.* As we know, Christ was inside the tomb when the stone was rolled away, so it could not have been him that was referred to as THE angel of the Lord. Besides, what purpose would God have in identifying Christ as an angel?

Secondly, angels are created beings, and I fail to see where one person of the Triune Godhead, creator of all things, should be identified as part of the creation, and thirdly, I feel that these are prayers that have already been answered. God answers prayers immediately unless there is a specific reason for delay; He does not store them away to be brought up at a later date. The purpose of bringing them to the forefront at this time is to show justification for the judgments to come, much as an indictment is read at the beginning of a trial. Another explanation might be that they are the prayers of those souls that John saw during the fifth seal, who were questioning when their deaths would be avenged, and God was demonstrating to them that they were to be answered shortly.

We see the angel dip the censer into the fire of the altar and fling this fire upon the earth. This is a distinct signal that judgment is about to begin.

THE SEVEN TRUMPETS

6. And the seven angels which had the seven trumpets prepared themselves to sound.

We now are at the point where judgment is imminent. God has given ample warning, has waited patiently for mankind to repent, and has no other choice than to proceed. The seven angels are prepared to blow their trumpets.

I believe that the trumpet judgments and the vial judgments come at the end of the tribulation period, and the tempo is speeded up so that one event immediately follows the one preceding. God's judgment will be swift and sure, and once it begins there will be little time for repentance. It will be practically too late.

While many will be saved during the tribulation period, they will endure severe hardships for their beliefs, or suffer death, or both. Accepting Christ now, during the church age, before the rapture of the church, is a far less painful way to enter into eternal bliss. We shall be spared the unspeakable hardships of the tribulation.

7. The first angel sounded, and there followed hail and fire mingled with blood, and they were cast upon the earth: and a third part of trees was burnt up, and all green grass was burnt up.

The first trumpet sounds and hail and fire mingled with blood are cast upon the earth. Now one might conceive of hail and fire being a terrible thunderstorm, but how can such a one explain the blood by any natural means? Mankind can only deduce that this is a direct act of an angry God. A third part of the trees and all the grass are burned up. There is a theory that the trees stand for leaders and the grass for the common people, but this is pure speculation of which I dare not partake. What could be wrong with interpreting the passage literally as written? Such an event would surely result in a monumental burden on mankind, both physically and mentally, and would be in keeping with God's purpose so what could be the reason for reading into it any more than what it says?

8. And the second angel sounded and as it were a great mountain burning with fire was cast into the sea; and the third part of the sea became blood;
9. and the third part of the creatures which were in the sea, and had life, died; and the third part of the ships were destroyed.

Once again, there can be no natural explanation for this event. It is clearly a supernatural act of God. I can visualize no natural event that could cause such horrendous damage. Some try to explain the "great mountain burning with fire" as a huge meteorite, but any meteorite large enough to cause a third of the sea creatures to die would probably hurl the earth off into outer space. We should not try to explain the workings of God in natural ways. God is not natural, he is supernatural, and his judgments will be supernatural events.

10. And the third angel sounded, and there fell a great star from Heaven, burning as it were a lamp, and it fell upon a third part of the rivers, and upon the fountains of waters;
11. And the name of the star is called wormwood: and a third part of the waters became wormwood; and many men died of the waters because they were made bitter.

Once again we see an event that can only be described as supernatural. A great fiery star falls from Heaven upon one third of all fresh water sources and its name is called wormwood.

Wormwood is a bush that is common to the Middle East and its taste is very bitter. Its sap is poisonous, causing convulsions, paralysis, and death. For it to be distributed over such a large area definitely points to divine action. We read in the text that many men died of the waters.

12. And the fourth angel sounded, and the third part of the sun was smitten, and the third part of the moon, and the third part of the stars; so as the third part of them was darkened, and the day shone not for a third part of it, and the night likewise.

Here we see yet another supernatural event; a third part of the sun, moon and stars is smitten. It does not take a rocket scientist to understand that if the sun suddenly lost one third of its power, a cataclysmic total destruction of the universe would most probably occur. This would at least create a temperature drop of magnanimous proportions, instantly destroying all life. How God is going to do this without destroying the universe is beyond my power of understanding, but that it shall happen, exactly as envisioned, I have absolutely no doubt.

THE WARNING

13. And I beheld, and heard an angel flying through the midst of Heaven, saying with a loud voice Woe, woe, woe, to the inhabiters of the earth by reason of the other voices of the trumpet of the three angels, which are yet to sound.

God's judgments up to this point while awesome and fear instilling, have more effect on man's environment than on his person. While some great numbers have perished, this pales when compared with the judgments to come. We see an angel flying over the earth announcing this fact. The severity of God's judgment will be like nothing man has ever seen, nor could even envision. The next three judgments are called woes.

CHAPTER 9

1. And the fifth angel sounded, and I saw a star fall from Heaven unto the earth: and to him was given the key of the bottomless pit.

2. And he opened the bottomless pit; and there arose a smoke out of the pit, as the smoke of a great furnace; and the sun and the air were darkened by reason of the smoke of the pit.

3. And there came out of the smoke locusts upon the earth: and unto them was given power, as the scorpions of the earth have power.

4. And it was commanded them that they should not hurt the grass of the earth, neither any green thing, neither any tree; but only those men which have not the seal of God in their foreheads.

5. And to them it was given that they should not kill them, but that they should be tormented five months: and their torment was as the torment of a scorpion, when he striketh a man.

6. And in those days shall men seek death, and shall not find it; and shall desire to die, and death shall flee from them.

7. And the shapes of the locusts were like unto horses prepared for battle; and on their heads were as it were crowns like gold, and their faces were as the faces of men.

8. And they had hair as the hair of women, and their teeth were as the teeth of lions,

9. And they had breastplates, as it were breastplates of iron; and the sound of their wings was as the sound of chariots of many horses running in battle.

10. And they had tails like unto scorpions, and there were stings in their tails: and their power was to hurt men five months.

11. And they had a king over them which is the angel of the bottomless pit, whose name in the Hebrew tongue is Abaddon, but in the Greek tongue hath his name Apollyon.

12. One woe is past; and behold, there come two woes more hereafter.

(THE FIRST WOE)

A star fell from Heaven. Apparently this star represents a person: (to HIM was given the key to the bottomless pit). There is not enough evidence to determine the identity of this person, nor is his identity necessary to understanding the vision.

The bottomless pit is opened and we see a horde of hideous creatures emerging to torment men for five months. John calls them locusts, but judging from their description, this identification must be considered symbolic. I believe there is a comparison in that their number was so great that they swarmed in great clouds as locusts do, and their torment lasted for five months, which is the normal lifespan of a locust. While these creatures seem to be a part of satan's realm, note that they are under the control of God. He restricts their activity to just what will serve his purpose. They are only allowed to torment, not kill, and they are restricted from touching those who are sealed in their forehead, the one hundred and forty four thousand sealed in chapter seven.

This prohibition also serves to prove that the one hundred and forty four thousand are still on the earth. The torment of these creatures is so great that men will seek death and shall not find it. Just as a comparison, consider receiving multiple scorpion stings constantly for a five month period. Normally, a man would be dead before the first day was over. Excruciating pain cannot begin to describe it. WARNING! All who fail to accept Christ as their savior while there is still time WILL go through these judgments.

13. And the sixth angel sounded, and I heard a voice from the four horns of the golden altar which is before God,
14. Saying to the sixth angel which had the trumpet, loose the four angels which are bound in the great river Euphrates.
15. And the four angels were loosed, which were prepared for an hour, and a day, and a month, and a year, for to slay the third part of men.
16. And the number of the army of the horsemen were two hundred thousand thousand: and I heard the number of them.

17. And thus I saw the horses in a vision, and them that sat on them, having breastplates of fire, and of Jacinth, and brimstone: and the heads were as the heads of lions; and out of their mouths issued fire and smoke and brimstone.

18. By these three was a third part of men killed, by the fire, and by the smoke, and by the brimstone, which issued out of their mouths.

19. For their power is in their mouth, and in their tails: for their tails were like unto serpents, and had heads, and with them they do hurt.

20. And the rest of the men which were not killed by these plagues yet repented not of the works of their hands, that they should not worship devils, and idols of gold, and silver, and brass, and stone, and of wood: which neither can see, nor hear, nor walk:

21. Neither repented they of their murders, nor of their sorceries, nor of their fornication, nor of their thefts.

THE SIXTH TRUMPET (SECOND WOE)

John sees four angels who were bound in the great river Euphrates. These angels were prepared for a special purpose of leading a two hundred million man army, but were restrained by God until the proper time. At present, the only country capable of coming up with an army of that size is China, but if the four leaders are to come from the area of the Euphrates, China would not seem to qualify.

The fact that there are four leaders instead of one, and the leaders come from the region of the Euphrates, could possibly indicate a coalition of Arab nations. At present, there are approximately 1.3 billion Muslims worldwide, with the majority of these centered around the area of the river Euphrates, so the numbers for such an army does exist. The task of supplying such an army with the essential beans, bullets, and band-aids, however, would be practically impossible for any world power today, and the cooperation necessary to form such a coalition of Muslim nations is nonexistent at present.

Judging by the description of the soldiers of this army I find it comfortable to believe in the possibility that they are not even human, but some form of creature, designed for this specific purpose. They quite possibly might be the fallen angels who followed satan. The description of the horses and the riders is quite different from the ordinary, so the riders may not even be normal men.   While most people assume they are human beings, I do not make that assumption.   I believe that this army will be assembled, furnished, and led by the four angels, but only when God determines that the time is right to release them to battle.

The text reads that a third of men would be killed.   This will be a catastrophe never before experienced in the history of the world, and be completed in a very short time rather than a long drawn out war.   The swiftness of this judgment will make it even more shocking, but as we read in verse 20, and 21, the people who remain still will not repent.

THE ANGEL, THE BOOK, THE TEMPLE, AND THE WITNESSES

Now, just as we did between the sixth and seventh seal, we come to an interlude between the sixth and seventh trumpet, when John sees a series of visions unrelated to the trumpet judgments time-line.

CHAPTER 10

1. And I saw another mighty angel come down from Heaven, clothed with a cloud;
and a rainbow was upon his head, and his face as it were the sun, and his feet as pillars of fire:
2.   and he had in his hand a little book open: and he set his right foot upon the sea and his left foot on the earth,
3. And cried with a loud voice, as when a lion roareth: and when he had cried, seven thunders uttered their voices.

THE ANGEL AND THE LITTLE BOOK

John sees a mighty angel come down from Heaven and stand with one foot on the land and the other on the sea.   In his hand is a little open book.   By his description he must be a special angel in the pattern of Michael or Gabriel, or perhaps even one of them.
Some scholars believe he is in fact Christ, but if that were true I believe that God would have identified him as Christ instead of an angel.   The action of placing his feet on the land and sea shows proprietorship and the little book is thought by many to contain the title deed to the universe.   I believe that the actions of this angel serve to notify the world that the millennial reign is soon to come.

I believe that the little book also contained information that was relative to John's work of publishing the book of revelations, as we will see in a later verse.

4. And when the seven thunders had uttered their voices, I was about to write: and heard a voice from Heaven saying unto me, seal up those things which the seven thunders uttered, and write them not.

THE SEVEN THUNDERS

John heard seven thunderous voices making proclamations that he was about to record when he was interrupted by a voice from Heaven saying: *seal up those things which the seven thunders uttered, and write them not.* It is evident that their messages were for John's understanding only. One can only speculate as to what they said.

5. *And the angel which I saw stand upon the sea and upon the earth lifted up his hand to Heaven,*
6. *And sware by him that liveth for ever and ever, who created Heaven, and the things which therein are, and the sea, and the things which are therein, that there should be time no longer:*
7. *But in the days of the voice of the seventh angel, when he shall begin to sound, the mystery of God should be finished, as he hath declared to his servants the prophets.*

THERE SHOULD BE TIME NO LONGER

The angel who held the book lifted his hand toward Heaven and swore by God that there should be time no longer.

This does not signal the end of time. Most scholars take this to mean there will be no more delay rather than time no longer. This verse, I believe, signifies the end of the effective rule of the antichrist. Though he is still on the earth, his seven year rule is nearly over, and his power is totally diminished. God is physically taking ownership so that he might personally foresee the rest of time. Perhaps this verse has a correlation with MAT 24:22 *And except those days be shortened, there should no flesh be saved: but for the elect's sake those days shall be shortened.* Also, see the explanation of the seventh trumpet.

8. *And the voice which I heard from heaven spake unto me again, and said, go and take the little book which is open in the hand of the angel which standeth upon the sea and upon the earth.*
9. *And I went unto the angel, and said unto him, give me the little book. And he said unto me, take it, and eat it up; and it shall make thy belly bitter, but it shall be in thy mouth sweet as honey.*

10. And I took the little book out of the angel's hand, and ate it up; and it was in my mouth sweet as honey, and as soon as I had eaten it, my belly was bitter.

THE LITTLE BOOK

John is given instructions from Heaven to take the little book from the angel and eat it. I don't know if he literally ate the book, but he certainly digested the information contained in it. I believe this knowledge was absorbed supernaturally and instantaneously. I believe that John was given to understand all of the visions that he recorded in the book. The revelation of Christ's ultimate and complete victory over the forces of evil is signified by the sweet taste, while the bitterness signifies the tremendous anguish caused by the necessary destruction of a portion of his creation at his own hand.

CHAPTER 11

1. And there was given me a reed like unto a rod: and the angel stood, saying, rise, and measure the temple of God, and the altar, and them that worship therein.

2. But the court which is without the temple leave out, and measure it not; for it is given unto the gentiles: and the holy city shall they tread under foot forty and two months.

THE MEASURING OF THE TEMPLE

The temple that John was told to measure did not exist at the time of this vision, nor does it exist today. The temple mount in Jerusalem today is occupied by a Muslim mosque. The last Jewish temple was destroyed in seventy A.D. by the Romans and has never been rebuilt.

I believe there will be two temples during the end times. First, the temple authorized by the antichrist in which he will allow the temple worship to be reinstated. Just when and where this new temple will be built is a mystery. Some students of prophesy have put forth the idea that this temple must be built before the tribulation can begin, but I believe that it will be one of the first acts of the antichrist after he takes office. The optimum location would of course, be it's original place, however, I fail to comprehend any scenario where the antichrist could possibly justify to the Muslim world the removal of the mosque that now occupies that location, without some miraculous intervention by God or even the devil. The only other alternative I can visualize is that it would be built at some nearby location considered to be a hallowed spot such as the garden of Gethsemane or the location of the ascension. In the beginning of the tribulation period, the antichrist will become a false friend to the nation of Israel. He will promise them protection from their enemies, and will provide it for the first three and one half years, at which time he will turn against them and assist their enemies. His most obnoxious act will be to desecrate the temple, and put an end to the daily worship.

Secondly will be the temple of the millennium which will be the seat of Christ. This may or may not be a new temple, but it may be the old temple, cleansed and rededicated. I believe that the temple John measures is the tribulation temple. I also believe that John sees this temple in the vision in its place in Jerusalem as he is told not to measure the outer court. One of the main reasons I believe this temple to be the tribulation temple, is that the gentiles will tread the outer court and the holy city for forty two months, (three and one half years). This corresponds to the last half of the tribulation period, when the antichrist will have desecrated the temple.

DAN 9:27   And he shall confirm the covenant with many for one week (generally understood to be the seven year tribulation period) *and in the midst of the week* (after three and one half years) *he shall cause the sacrifice and the oblation to cease, and for the overspreading of abominations he shall make it desolate, even until the consummation of the determined shall be poured out upon the desolate.*
DAN 11:31   And arms shall stand on his part, and they shall pollute the sanctuary of strength, and shall take away the daily sacrifice, and they shall place the abomination that maketh desolate.
DAN 12:11   And from the time that the daily sacrifice shall be taken away, and the abomination that maketh desolate set up, there shall be a thousand two hundred and ninety days.
MAT 24:15-16   When ye shall see the abomination of desolation spoken of by Daniel the prophet, stand in the holy place, (whoso readeth, let him understand) then let them which be in Judea flee into the mountain.

I believe that the abomination of desolation will be the image of the antichrist that will be produced by the false prophet, and installed in the holy of holies in the temple.

The reason that John is told to measure the inner temple is that even though it has been desecrated by the antichrist, it is still the property of the sovereign Christ. This act of measuring the temple, more than likely corresponds to the survey that is done in modern times when a property changes hands. Not only is the temple to become physically the property of Christ, but he is about to become the object of worship, replacing the antichrist.

What could make the antichrist change his direction so rapidly and drastically? The benevolent world leader who re-instituted the temple worship and daily sacrifice suddenly turns on the nation of Israel and persecutes them violently. It is my belief that after the battle between Michael and the angels on the one side, and satan and his angels on the other, (described in chapter twelve), that satan and the antichrist strike a deal. The devil, furious over his defeat and banishment from access to Heaven, now turns his vitriolic anger against the apple of God's eye, the nation of Israel. The antichrist, with his thirst for power and dominance becomes a willing ally in the devils cause.

There are documented instances where individuals or even groups of individuals have claimed to have entered a pact with the devil and seem to have benefited from it. Several rock music groups immediately come to my mind. The devil, with his glib promises is extremely appealing to the worldly person, who is no match for the devil's chicanery. While a deal with the devil will usually bring temporal benefits, the price of these benefits is the eternal soul!

3. And I will give power unto my two witnesses, and they shall prophesy a thousand two hundred and three score days, clothed in sackcloth.
4. These are the two olive trees, and the two candlesticks standing before the God of the earth.
5. And if any man will hurt them, fire proceedeth out of their mouth, and devoureth their enemies: and if any man will hurt them, he must in this manner be killed.
6. These have power to shut heaven, that it rain not in the days of their prophesy: and have power over waters to turn them to blood, and to smite the earth with all plagues, as often as they will.
7. And when they shall have finished their testimony, the beast that ascendeth out of the bottomless pit shall make war against them, and shall overcome them, and kill them.

8. And their dead bodies shall lie in the street of the great city, which spiritually is called Sodom and Egypt, where also our Lord was crucified.

9. And they of the people and kindreds and tongues and nations shall see their dead bodies three days and an half, and shall not suffer their dead bodies to be put in graves.

10. And they that dwell upon the earth shall rejoice over them, and make merry, and shall send gifts one to another; because these two prophets tormented them that dwelt on the earth.

11. And after three days and an half the Spirit of life from God entered into them, and they stood upon their feet; and great fear fell upon them which saw them.

12. And they heard a great voice from Heaven saying unto them, come up hither.   And they ascended up to Heaven in a cloud; and their enemies beheld them.

13. And the same hour was there a great earthquake and the tenth part of the city fell, and in the earthquake were slain of men seven thousand: and the remnant were affrighted, and gave glory to the God of Heaven.

14. The second woe is past; and, behold, the third woe cometh quickly.

THE TWO WITNESSES

Much speculation has been offered as to the identity of the two witnesses.   Their identity is of no importance at this time.   God says that they are his two witnesses, and if we needed to know their identity, he would have provided it.   What is vastly more important than their identity is their works.   They are called witnesses therefore their mission is to spread the truth of God's word.   They are empowered by God to perform supernatural feats in order to validate the fact that they were truly sent by him.

Verse three states that they will prophesy for three and a half years, most probably the last half of the tribulation period.   At the end of this three and a half years, they will be killed and their bodies left unburied for three and a half days, after which they will miraculously stand up under their own power, and be transported into Heaven in a cloud, in front of many witnesses.

It always amazes me that even after so many manifestations of his power, and his just nature, many people still do not believe the truth of God.   At this time the city of Jerusalem has become so sinful that it is compared to Sodom, and Egypt. The act of destroying the two witnesses is not without consequence, however, as we read in verse 13: *And the same hour was there a great earthquake, and the tenth part of the city fell, and of the earthquake were slain of men seven thousand: and the remnant were affrighted and gave glory to the God of Heaven.* Whether this was a heartfelt repentance, or a temporary result of their fear, God only knows.

Some have brought forward the idea that the period between their death and subsequent resurrection (three and a half days) might stand for three and a half years just as the seven days in the book of Daniel stands for seven years, and they could not possibly be men as their bodies would decay in that length of time. Actually, if God wanted their bodies to lie for three and a half years without decaying, that would be child's play for him. They favor the possibility that the two witnesses, rather than being actual persons, might be concepts such as law and grace, or institutions such as the church and representative government. In the absence of any proper identification of the two witnesses in the scripture, to consider such ideas is pure speculation. The identity of the two witnesses is totally insignificant while their role is totally vital. Their actions and their circumstances however would certainly indicate that they in fact will be persons.

15. *And the seventh angel sounded, and there were great voices in Heaven, saying, the kingdoms of this world are become the kingdoms of our Lord, and of his Christ; and he shall reign for ever and ever.*
16. *And the four and twenty elders, which sat before God on their seats. Fell upon their faces, and worshipped God.*
17. *Saying, we give thee thanks, O Lord God Almighty, which art, and wast, and art to come; because thou hast taken to thee thy great power, and hast reigned.*
18. *And the nations were angry, and thy wrath is come, and the time of the dead, that they should be judged, And that thou shouldst give reward unto thy servants the prophets, and to the saints, and them that fear thy name, small and great; and shouldst destroy them that destroy the earth.*

THE SEVENTH TRUMPET (THIRD WOE)

The seventh angel sounds and thunderous voices from Heaven proclaim the Lordship of Christ. Nothing occurs on earth, so how can this be the third woe?

First, let us examine what this pronouncement means. Some scholars say it represents the beginning of the millennial reign, but I disagree with them, as there are still heathens on the earth, and saints in Heaven, and there are still judgments to come. I submit that this pronouncement proclaims the end of the rule of the antichrist. He is still on the earth, but his forces are in disarray, and he no longer maintains control. Christ will assume control and "clean-up" in preparation for the millennial kingdom. In these verses, coupled with the measuring of the temple, and the proclamation that there should be time no longer, the lordship of Christ is formally announced to the antichrist and the whole world.

Verse eighteen is a key to understanding where the third woe comes in. *And thy wrath is come* this verse announces that the final judgment of all mankind is imminent; therefore this is an anticipated woe for the damned; and anticipated reward for the saints.

19.   And the temple of God was opened in Heaven, and there was seen in his temple, the ark of his testament: and there were lightnings, and voices, and thunderings, and an earthquake, and great hail.

This verse fits in with the "taking over" of Christ at the sounding of the seventh trumpet. The thunders, voices, lightnings, earthquake, and hail profoundly announce the event. I believe that all the remaining inhabitants of the earth will be able to look up and see this when it happens. The opening of Heaven to visibility from earth is not a new event, as it has occurred on several previous occasions in the Bible, but these events were usually viewings by select individuals or groups only. The baptism of Jesus and the stoning of Stephen are examples of this phenomenon.

I believe that on this occasion, every remaining person on the earth will be literally forced to see this vision, and realize the seriousness of their calamity. This may even be the time that *every knee shall bow, and every tongue confess that Jesus Christ is Lord.*

CHAPTER 12

1. And there appeared a great wonder in Heaven; A woman clothed with the sun, and the moon under her feet, and upon her head a crown of twelve stars:
2. And she being with child cried, travailing in birth, and pained to be delivered.
3 And there appeared another wonder in Heaven, and behold, a great red dragon, having seven heads and ten horns, and seven crowns upon his heads.
4. And his tail drew the third part of the stars of Heaven, and did cast them to the earth: and the dragon stood before the woman which was ready to be delivered, for to devour her child as soon as it was born.
5. And she brought forth a man child, who was to rule all nations with a rod of iron: and her child was caught up unto God, and to his throne.
6. And the woman fled into the wilderness, where she hath a place prepared of God, that they should feed her there a thousand two hundred and threescore days,

THE WOMAN CLOTHED WITH THE SUN

To understand who the woman is, we must first look to verse five. And she brought forth a man child, who was to rule all nations with a rod of iron: and her child was caught up into God and his throne. There can be no doubt that this man child is Jesus Christ and no other. If the man child is Christ, then who could the woman be?

Some scholars say the church, but I disagree. The church was born of Christ, not Christ of the church. Others say the Virgin Mary, but she does not fit the text of verse six.

We find several clues to the woman's identity in verse six and in Mathew chapter twenty four.

Verse six reads: *And the woman fled into the wilderness, where she hath a place prepared of God, that they should feed her there a thousand two hundred and threescore days.*

I find this figure of a thousand two hundred and threescore days to be fascinating. That is the exact number of days in three and a half years, (using the Hebrew calendar of thirty day months) which corresponds beautifully with the last half of the tribulation period.

Mathew 24:15-16 *When ye therefore shall see the abomination of desolation, spoken of by Daniel the prophet, (whoso readeth let him understand) then let them which be in Judea flee into the mountains.* The text of chapter twenty four goes on to tell them to flee in utmost haste, not going back into their house for anything.

Who was to flee? Them which be in Judea. I therefore submit that the woman is the nation of Israel (Judea).

We have already established that during the middle of the tribulation, the antichrist will desecrate the temple (the abomination of desolation) and for the next thousand two hundred and threescore days (verse six), he will persecute the woman (Israel) but God will protect her.

THE GREAT DRAGON

The dragon identified in verses three and four must surely be satan himself. While his hatred and animosity are directed at God, he realizes that a direct assault would be disastrous, so he acts deviously by attempting to destroy God's creation. As an eternal being, having direct knowledge of God's work, he knows that by destroying the man-child he would be in fact destroying a third part of the Triune Godhead. Not being able to destroy the eternal Christ of Heaven, when he saw Christ become flesh and dwell amongst us, he thought, "what an opportunity; Christ in the flesh is now vulnerable!" In fact, he probably thought he had succeeded when Christ was crucified; what a let down when he was resurrected! I believe the resurrection is depicted in the last part of verse five: Her child was caught up unto God and to his throne.

A number of years pass between verse five and verse six. Verse five deals with the resurrection of Christ; verse six deals with the middle of the tribulation period.

7. *And there was war in Heaven: Michael and his angels fought against the dragon; and the dragon fought and his angels,*

8. *And prevailed not; neither was their place found any more in Heaven.*

9. *And the great dragon was cast out, that old serpent, called the devil, and Satan, which deceiveth the whole world: he was cast out into the earth, and his angels were cast out with him.*

10. *And I heard a loud voice saying in Heaven, now is come salvation, and strength, and the kingdom of our God, and the power of his Christ: for the accuser of our brethren is cast down, which accused them before our God day and night.*

11. *And they overcame him by the blood of the Lamb, and by the word of their testimony; and they loved not their lives unto the death.*

12. *Therefore rejoice, ye Heavens, and ye that dwell in them. Woe to the inhabiters of the earth and of the sea! For the devil is come down unto you, having great wrath, because he knoweth that he hath but a short time.*

13. *And when the dragon saw that he was cast unto the earth, he persecuted the woman which brought forth the man child.*

14. *And to the woman were given two wings of a great eagle, that she might fly into the wilderness, into her place, where she is nourished for a time, and times, and half a time, from the face of the serpent.*

15. *And the serpent cast out of his mouth water as a flood after the woman, that he might cause her to be carried away of the flood.*

16. *And the earth helped the woman, and the earth opened her mouth, and swallowed up the flood which the dragon cast out of his mouth.*

17. *And the dragon was wroth with the woman, and went to make war with the remnant of her seed, which keep the commandments of God, and have the testimony of Jesus Christ.*

WAR IN HEAVEN

As a child I was taught that satan was banished from Heaven before the creation. I believed this for many years until I began to prayerfully study the Bible in depth. Not wanting to believe that I could be wrong, I frantically searched for the particulars that would validate this belief. I came to the conclusion that he has never been denied access to Heaven up until the present. I know that some of you who were taught the same thing that I was will say: What about the fall of Lucifer in Isaiah 14:12? *How art thou fallen O Lucifer, son of the morning! How art thou cut down to the ground, which did weaken the nations?*

How about LUKE 10-18 *And he said unto them: I beheld satan as lightning, fall from Heaven?*

I submit that this first "fall" was spiritual rather than physical. While some limitations were placed on satan's use of his powers, his access to Heaven was not denied.

I submit JOB 2:1 as evidence: *Again there was a day when the sons of God came to present themselves before the Lord and satan came also among them to present himself before the Lord.*

We see then, that satan still had access in Job's day, and if we look at verse ten, we see that he is called the accuser of the brethren, so it seems that even though satan may have been restricted to some degree, he still has sufficient access to accuse the brethren day and night.

While we are on the subject of satan's capabilities, I would like to clear up a couple of misconceptions that are widely shared by believers and non-believers alike. Most people picture satan and his demons abiding in hell, and coming out to do battle with God by attacking his creation. I believe that while satan knows all about hell, and realizes that it will be his final home, he has not yet been there, doesn't want to go there, and when he finally goes he will probably be screaming all the way like a condemned man heading for the gallows.

The second misconception is the belief that satan can be everywhere at once. In theological terms, that is called omnipresence. Omnipresence is a capability reserved for God, and practiced by God only. A very costly error that many Christians make when believing (erroneously) in the omnipresence of satan is to say "the devil made me do it", when in reality, he was probably far away at the time. When we blame satan for our sins, we are denying our own culpability, thus making us ineligible for forgiveness!

I JOHN 1:8-9: *If we say that we have no sin, we deceive ourselves and the truth is not in us. If we confess our sins, he is faithful and just to forgive us our sins, and to cleanse us from all unrighteousness.* (Emphasis on the second "IF"). Only by accepting full responsibility for my sins, by not trying to excuse my behavior, not trying to shift the blame or any part of it to any other, can I receive full forgiveness. Failure to accept responsibility is rampant today, even among some devout Christians! If satan can fool them into shifting the blame, he can negate their forgiveness.

In verses seven and eight, we see the first step in the final judgment of satan. Michael, the archangel, and all the angels of Heaven fight against satan and his demons. His demons are almost exclusively believed to be those angels who followed him in rebellion, and also believed to be: the third part of the stars of Heaven, spoken of in verse four. Now here's a comforting thought. If one third of the angels in Heaven followed satan, then for every demon he has, God has two angels. Hallelujah!

Now if we combine all the clues from chapter twelve, we see that this war spoken of in verse seven most probably occurs in the middle of the tribulation period. Satan is finally completely banished from Heaven, and goes on a rampage against the apple of God's eye, the remnant of the nation of Israel. He finds a willing ally in the antichrist.

CHAPTER 13

1. And I stood upon the sand of the sea, and saw a beast rise up out of the sea, having seven heads and ten horns, and upon his horns ten crowns, and upon his heads the name of blasphemy.

2. And the beast I saw was like unto a leopard, and his feet were as the feet of a bear, and his mouth as the mouth of a lion, and the dragon gave him his power, and his seat, and great authority.

3. And I saw one of his heads as it were wounded to death; and his deadly wound was healed: and all the world wondered after the beast.

4. And they worshipped the dragon which gave power unto the beast: and they worshipped the beast saying who is like unto the beast? Who is able to make war with him?

5. And there was given unto him a mouth speaking great things and blasphemies; and power was given unto him to continue forty and two months.

6. And he opened his mouth in blasphemy against God, to blaspheme his name, and his tabernacle, and them that dwell in Heaven.

7. And it was given unto him to make war with the saints, and to overcome them: and power was given unto him over all kindreds, and tongues, and nations.

8. And all that dwell upon the earth shall worship him, whose names are not written in the book of life of the Lamb slain from the foundation of the world.

9. If any man have an ear, let him hear.

10. He that leadeth into captivity shall go into captivity: he that killeth with the sword must be killed with the sword. Here is the patience and the faith of the saints.

THE BEAST FROM THE SEA (THE ANTICHRIST)

John sees a beast rise up from the sea. This beast bears a remarkable resemblance to the vision seen by the prophet Daniel in Daniel, chapter seven. The only difference is that Daniel saw four beasts, one resembling a LION, one resembling a BEAR, one resembling a LEOPARD and the fourth beast, dreadful and terrible with great iron teeth and ten horns, while the beast that John saw was one beast, having body parts from a LEOPARD, a BEAR, and a LION, and the beast himself compares to Daniel's fourth beast. This difference can be easily explained.

In Daniels vision, each beast represented a different kingdom; each was dominant at a different time. The lion represented Babylon, the bear represented the Medo-Persian Empire, the leopard represented Greece, and the fourth beast represented the Roman Empire, which eventually assimilated the territories of the other three.

In John's vision, the beast represents the antichrist, which will revive and combine all these other kingdoms at the same time, thus the single beast rather than the four separate ones. John's beast, like Daniel's, has ten horns.

I can see far too many similarities between these two visions for anyone to claim that they are not related. Is it not amazing that two men, separated by hundreds of years, would see and record the same vision in such detail? Methinks I see the hand of God!

Herein we see one of the keys to understanding the mysteries of the book of revelations. Many of the visions relate back to similar visions of the Old Testament prophets. In looking at history, we can see where and how these former visions came to fruition, and gain an insight to understanding the corresponding vision in the book of revelations. This amazing correlation between men's prophesies, separated by hundreds of years, also tends to prove their origin as divine, rather than the imagination of the authors.

In verse two, we see where the antichrist will be empowered by satan (the dragon). Remember, we are most probably back to the middle of the tribulation period, and God is still allowing satan, the antichrist, and sinful man free reign for the next three and one half years. The antichrist will be free to rule as he chooses, with some feeble resistance from the followers of Christ.

Of course, God's witnesses will be a thorn in his side, (the one hundred and forty four thousand, and the two witnesses from chapter eleven), but his power will be virtually un-challenged until the end of the tribulation. Just as Hitler did in WWII, he will use the persecution of the Jews as a focal point for rallying his forces.

Of course some may believe that the antichrist's "deal with the devil" comes at the beginning of the tribulation, but I believe it comes in the middle, which would account for the antichrist's abrupt change in direction and attitude. Another clue to this fact is found in verse five: power was given unto him to continue forty and two months. This could only mean the last half of the tribulation period. This also suggests that this power was given to him by the devil.

The seven heads and ten horns are further identified in chapter seventeen, but for now it is sufficient to know that they represent nations that will swear allegiance to the antichrist and will do his bidding.

The name of blasphemy from verse one, which is located on the seven heads, is most probably the name of the antichrist, or some form of logo with the name of his kingdom in it, or both.

The head with the deadly wound that is healed represents the revived Roman Empire. This also is further explained in chapter seventeen.

The revived Roman Empire will not be named as such but it will encompass all the territories of the original and then some. It will have the same form of empirical government as the old empire, with the antichrist at its head.

In verses four through six we see that worship of satan and the antichrist will be commonplace as well as blasphemy against God.

While the inhabitants of the earth during this period must surely realize who God is, what he is doing, and what he is about to do, (He maintains powerful witnesses during this period), they will openly and brazenly defy him. It is no wonder that their actions culminate in their damnation.

In verses seven through ten, the forces of the antichrist subdue the whole earth. There will be a remnant of believers who can only survive by depending on the divine providence of God, through patience and faith. They are warned to not depend on carnal methods. What a tremendous burden the believers who endure the tribulation will be forced to bear! I shudder to think of it. Oh, how glad that I am saved from such woe, through the blood of Jesus Christ, my savior!

11. And I beheld another beast coming up out of the earth; and he had two horns like a lamb, and he spake as a dragon.

12. And he exerciseth all the power of the first beast before him, and causeth the earth and them which dwell therein to worship the first beast, whose deadly wound was healed.

13. And he doeth great wonders, so that he maketh fire come down from Heaven on the earth in the sight of men,

14. And deceiveth them that dwell on the earth by the means of those miracles which he had power to do in the sight of the beast; saying to them that dwell on the earth, that they should make an image to the beast, which had the wound by a sword, and did live.

15. And he had power to give life unto the image of the beast, that the image of the beast should both speak, and cause that as many as would not worship the image of the beast should be killed.

16. And he causeth all both small and great, rich and poor, free and bond, to receive a mark in their right hand, or in their foreheads:

17. And that no man might buy or sell, save he that had the mark, or the name of the beast, or the number of his name.

18 Here is wisdom. Let him that hath understanding count the number of the beast: for it is the number of a man; and his number is six hundred three score and six.

THE SECOND BEAST

The second beast is thought to be an apostate Jew, who follows the antichrist. The reason for this belief is that he comes from the earth, while the first beast comes from the sea. Some scholars believe the sea represents the gentile masses, while the earth represents the Promised Land, home of God's chosen people. While this is a commonly accepted belief, I find no proof in scripture; therefore I will make no comment.

This second beast received power from the first beast. The second beast does great wonders and deceives the earth's inhabitants. He and the antichrist will be operating under the power of satan. The only power that satan has is that which God allows him to have. While he is capable of counterfeiting all the miracles of God, he has no control over the breath of life. He can neither create life, nor destroy it except by the will of God. I submit the story of Job as evidence of this.

The second beast then convinces his followers to make an image of the first beast, and he causes that image to speak. It would seem as though he were acting as the antichrist's high priest. He demands that the image be worshipped.

It is this second beast that requires everyone to take the infamous "mark of the beast". At this point, all those who refuse the mark will become non-existent for all practical purposes. They will have no rights, and be forced to become fugitives.

I would daresay that no other subject in the book of revelations has received more scrutiny or notoriety than the "mark". One has only to mention the book of revelations and most of the listeners thoughts automatically turn to the mark of the beast. There has been a great deal of speculation about the mark, most of it merely adding to the confusion. Verses seventeen and eighteen provide all the information about the mark that we are going to get. In them we see three possibilities: (1) The mark, (2) The name of the beast, (3) The number of his name.

Normally, when an author lists a series of options as in verse seventeen, it is because he does not know for sure which one applies. As God is the author of the book of revelations, this could not possibly be true in this case. The only other reason I can see for God to list three different variations of the mark, is that there WILL BE three different variations of the mark! Some will have the mark, some will have the name of the beast, and some will have the number of his name. I know there will probably be some who disagree with me, but that's how it reads. I didn't believe in three variations either until I did this study, but there it is, plain as day, in God's inspired word!

What I believe to be a widely circulated myth about the mark is the fact that many believe it will be an individual serial number for identification purposes. Some Christians are suspicious of ATM cards, credit cards, and bank account numbers. I know of one Christian who denounced his social security number in a classified ad, for fear that it might be the mark of the beast, and I have heard of others doing the same thing. Such paranoia is totally unwarranted. The mark of the beast will come during the tribulation period, not before. I believe that it, in fact, will not come until the middle of the tribulation. The only reason for a present Christian to be concerned about the mark is if they plan on missing the rapture! Actually, I don't think you even have a choice, if you're saved, you're going.

While there will most probably be personal identification numbers assigned during the reign of the antichrist, these numbers alone will not be the mark of the beast. HOWEVER, this ID number will most surely have the mark along with it, whether it be a bar code, a chip inserted under the skin, or a tattoo. Therefore, if one accepts the ID number, they will most probably be accepting the mark of the beast also. But not to worry about our current system, the mark of the beast will not be instituted until the tribulation period, so keep your ATM cards if you so desire.

CHAPTER 14

1. And I looked, and, lo, a Lamb stood on the mount Sion, and with him an hundred forty and four thousand, having his Father's name written in their foreheads.
2. And I heard a voice from Heaven, as the voice of many waters, and as the voice of a great thunder: and I heard the voice of harpers harping with their harps:
3. And they sung as it were a new song before the throne, and before the four beasts, and the elders: and no man could learn that song but the hundred and forty and four thousand, which were redeemed from the earth.
4. These are they which were not defiled with women; for they are virgins. These are they which follow the Lamb whither-soever he goeth. These were redeemed from among men, being the firstfruits unto God and to the Lamb.
5. And in their mouth was found no guile: for they are without fault before the throne of God.

THE VICTORY SONG

Christ, the Lamb of God, is standing on earth with the one hundred and forty four thousand from chapter seven, and the one hundred and forty four thousand are singing a song that is peculiar to them only. I believe this is a victory song as well as a joyous song of praise for God keeping them through the tribulation period. Note that their number is not diminished. For this group to come through unscathed is indeed a miracle, considering that they were ministering for Christ, against the antichrist.

The reason their song is unique to them, only they could appreciate the depth of their experience and their divine protection through it all.

All Heaven is attentive to their singing. Verse three tells us that they are redeemed from the earth. If this means they are translated to Heaven, (as I think it does), what triumphant entrance they must make! What marvelous tales they have to tell the Heavenly Hosts!

The description of their character reveals that only through total abstinence from worldly pursuits can one develop the faith, perseverance, and focus to serve to the degree that they were called upon to serve. The greater distance we maintain between us and the world, the greater our nearness to God. I am not suggesting that every believer should live the totally dedicated life that was led by the one hundred and forty four thousand, nor does God demand it of us, but on the other side of the coin, we must be prepared to make that sacrifice if we are called upon by God to perform in the special way that they were called to.

Here I would like to inject a thought about forced celibacy. One need only look at the history of forced celibacy to see that it has been highly detrimental to the Kingdom of God, especially to the church. I COR 7:8-9 *I say therefore to the unmarried and widows, it is good for them if they abide even as I. But if they cannot contain, let them marry: for it is better to marry than to burn.* We see here as God speaks through the apostle Paul, that God prefers celibacy in his servants, but does not demand it.

We have seen Christ and the one hundred and forty four thousand standing on the earth, in the city of Jerusalem, singing their victory song. This serves as an opening scene for a new phase in the coming events. Christ is now on the earth, and the despotic rule of the antichrist is now over, although he and his followers are still a dire threat to God's people.

Three of Heaven's angels issue proclamations to all on the earth. These are prophetic proclamations of events that are to occur next. God is always open and aboveboard in his dealings with mankind, forever giving more than ample warning of his future plans. These warnings also serve to inform the believers so that they will know what to expect.

6. And I saw another angel fly in the midst of Heaven, having the everlasting gospel to preach unto them that dwell on the earth, and to every nation, and kindred, and tongue, and people.

7. Saying with a loud voice, fear God, and give glory to him; for the hour of his judgment is come: and worship him that made heaven, and earth, and the sea, and the fountains of waters.

THE ANGEL AND THE GOSPEL

God's tribulation witnesses have been proclaiming the gospel up to this point, and now we see the gospel being proclaimed directly from Heaven. This proclamation verifies that the message of the witnesses was truly from God, and that it was truth. This is yet another plea for mankind to repent, and an explanation of justification for judgment. ISA 55:11 *So shall my word be that goeth forth out of my mouth; it shall not return unto me void, but it shall accomplish that which I please, and it shall prosper in the thing whereto I sent it.* God never uses idle words as some of his creation has been known to do. He always has a purpose for his speech, and that purpose is never thwarted. No one on judgment day will be able to truthfully say "I didn't know."

8. And there followed another angel saying, Babylon is fallen, is fallen, that great city, because she made all nations drink of the wine of the wrath of her fornication.

BABYLON IS FALLEN

Not physical Babylon, but spiritual Babylon. Sin centered, morally corrupt, apostate Babylon in the guise of the antichrist and his kingdom. The Babylon spoken of in the book of revelations represents a religious system that dates all the way back to the tower of Babel, on the plane of Shinar, in the book of Genesis, chapters ten and eleven. The tower of Babel was a turning point in mankind's relationship to his creator.

Up to that point, man, although plagued by his sinful nature, had for the most part, a desire to please God, and to accept his lordship. At a certain point, the seeds of rebellion grew into an attempt to produce a Godless system. This system has as its basis, man's assumed right to question God, to defy God, even to disobey God! This assumption is the height of apostasy. This system has been propagated by satan throughout the ages and is still alive in the kingdom of the antichrist.

The antichrist had by coercion, brute force, and false promises, drawn all the nations of the earth into spiritual adultery. While the time for his total destruction is not yet, Christ is now in control and the antichrist most surely knows that his days are numbered. His kingdom, already in decline, is about to be destroyed by the power of Christ before his very eyes.

9. *And the third angel followed them, saying with a loud voice, if any man worship the beast and his image and receive his mark in his forehead, or in his hand,*

10. *The same shall drink of the wine of the wrath of God, which is poured out without mixture into the cup of his indignation; and he shall be tormented with fire and brimstone in the presence of the holy angels, and in the presence of the Lamb:*

11. *And the smoke of their torment ascendeth up for ever and ever: and they have no rest day or night, who worship the beast and his image, and whosoever receiveth the mark of his name.*

12. *Here is the patience of the saints: here are they that keep the commandments of God, and the faith of Jesus.*

THE JUDGMENT OF HIS WORSHIPPERS

An angel proclaims in a loud voice that all who worship the beast or the image, or receive the mark, will be doomed to spend eternity in the lake of fire. Imagine their anguish when they see their once secure world falling apart, and then they hear this pronouncement of doom. I would most certainly not like to be in their shoes! Most however will continue to deny God. Sin, once tasted has a sweet, enticing, savor to the flesh, so compelling that the sinner will gladly overlook its cancerous effects on the soul.

13. *And I heard a voice from Heaven saying unto me, write, blessed are the dead which die in the Lord from henceforth: yea, saith the spirit, that they may rest from their labors; and their works do follow them.*

Blessed are the dead which die in the Lord from hence-forth. According to the way this verse reads, it is safe to assume that there are still some believers on the earth, and that their trials and tribulations are about to increase drastically. It had long been my belief that there would be no souls saved during the tribulation. The more I got into this study, the more convinced I became that I was wrong. The only way that one could die in the Lord would be to be a believer. Here we are near the end of the tribulation and God speaks of an increase in the terror. This is probably a last ditch effort by satan and the antichrist to exact as much damage as possible.

14. And I looked, and behold a white cloud, and upon the cloud one sat like unto the Son of man, having on his head a golden crown, and in his hand a sharp sickle.

15. And another angel came out of the temple, crying with a loud voice to him that sat on the cloud, thrust in thy sickle, and reap; for the harvest of the earth is ripe.

16. And he that sat on the cloud thrust in his sickle on the earth; and the earth was reaped.

17. And another angel came out of the temple which is in Heaven, he also having a sharp sickle.

18. And another angel came out from the altar, which had power over fire; and cried with a loud cry to him that had the sharp sickle, saying, thrust in thy sharp sickle, and gather in the clusters of the vine of the earth; for her grapes are fully ripe.

19. And the angel thrust in his sickle into the earth, and gathered the vine of the earth, and cast it into the great winepress of the wrath of God.

20. And the winepress was trodden without the city, and blood came out of the winepress, even unto the horse bridles, by the space of a thousand and six hundred furlongs.

THE HARVEST

Now we come to another vision that is difficult to understand. (At least for me it was.) I puzzled for days because I was operating under preconceived notions that were incorrect. First, I viewed this as a single event; and secondly I tried to place this event into a chronological time line at a certain point. Thirdly, I assumed that both the actions of Christ and of the angel were judgments against the lost. None of these notions looked right on paper. One thing that was deeply puzzling to me was the river of blood, four feet high and one hundred and eighty four miles long. For this to occur in a one time event would entail the destruction of nearly every man that ever lived, yet there were millions destroyed prior to this vision, and there are to be millions destroyed after it. In frustration, I forced myself to abandon all thought about this and seek God's guidance.

The very next day, I woke up with the answer. I believe this vision is symbolic of the total collective harvest of mankind. The two main characters in this vision are Christ and an angel. This angel may even be the devil himself. The vision of Christ with the sickle represents the harvest of the saved, rather than the lost. The raptured church is already in Heaven, as well as the twenty four elders, the two witnesses, and the tribulation martyrs. There are, however still some believers on the earth. We have now come to the end of God's judgments with the coming of the seven vials and these last judgments are too horrible for these believers to withstand, so many of them are removed to Heaven so as not to have to endure it. It is most probable that they are taken in death, as envisioned by the reaping with a sickle. There are two verses that cause me to believe this. I COR 15:50 *Now this I say brethren, that flesh and blood cannot inherit the kingdom of God:* HEB 9:27 *And as it is appointed unto men once to die, but after this the judgment.* That is why I believe they will be taken by death. A real Christian should never fear death; in fact, they should prefer it over life in a totally apostate society. The believers who are left behind will be divinely protected from these last judgments.

The vision of the angel with the sickle represents the harvest of the lost. I believe the river of blood alludes to the final great battle of Armageddon.

I believe the term "treading of the winepress", to be symbolic of the terrible carnage of that battle; a degree of carnage heretofore unseen in the history of the universe. This term is also used in old testament prophesy. While I have no doubt that God could produce a winepress large enough to hold all of his enemies at one time, I see no reason for him to produce such a theatrical display. Also, if we skip forward to the battle of Armageddon in chapter nineteen, we see that the remainder of the followers of satan are slain by the sword of Christ, and their flesh is eaten by the fowls of the air. This would not seem to be the treading of a winepress. Chapter nineteen does read however that Christ is to tread the wine-press of the wrath of God, so that would tend to link this vision of the angel with the sickle to the battle of Armageddon.

While there may be a literal river of blood at the battle of Armageddon, (and I suspect there will be), It is my belief that this river will stem from a semi-traditional battle rather than the treading of a winepress. This battle, however, as I explain later is one where Christ needs only to speak victory, and it immediately comes to pass.

THE SEVEN VIALS

In chapters fifteen and sixteen we see the final judgments of God on sinful mankind. These judgments are so terrible that it would seem that no one could survive. Just the effect on the water alone, would be enough to destroy all living beings. There will be not one drop of drinkable water, and man could not normally live more than a few days without water. There will, however, be enough survivors that satan is able to muster a sizeable army at the battle of Armageddon. When we consider how total the seven vial judgments are, we must conclude that God purposely keeps them alive, in grave distress, so that they have to endure the entirety of his judgments. Even those who desire death cannot secure it. I am equally sure that the believers who are left on the earth are divinely protected from these plagues.

CHAPTER 15

1. And I saw another sign in Heaven, great and marvelous, seven angels having the seven last plagues; for in them is filled up the wrath of God.

2. And I saw as it were a sea of glass mingled with fire: and them that had gotten the victory over the beast, and over his image, and over his mark, and over the number of his name, stand on the sea of glass, having the harps of God.

3. And they sing the song of Moses the servant of God, and the song of the Lamb, saying, great and marvelous are thy works, Lord God Almighty; just and true are thy ways, thou King of saints.

4. Who shall not fear thee, O Lord, and glorify thy name? For thou only art holy: for all the nations shall come and worship before thee; for thy judgments are made manifest.

5. And after that I looked, and, behold, the temple of the tabernacle of the testimony in Heaven was opened:

6. And the seven angels came out of the temple, having the seven plagues, clothed in pure and white linen, and having their breasts girded with golden girdles.

7. And one of the four beasts gave unto the seven angels seven golden vials full of the wrath of God, who liveth for ever and ever.

8. And the temple was filled with smoke from the glory of God, and from his power; and no man was able to enter into the temple, till the seven plagues of the seven angels were fulfilled.

PREPARATION

The location is Heaven. The scene is described by John as great and marvelous. We see the tribulation saints singing praises to God as they play their harps in accompaniment. We know they are the tribulation saints because they have overcome the beast, his mark, his image, and the number of his name. By this, we know that they have been on the earth through the last half of the tribulation.

It is my belief that most of the saints are in Heaven at this point, but if we look at the warning in chapter 16, verse 15; this is a warning to believers, so there are still some on earth.

The sea of glass, mingled with fire, speaks of the splendor of Heaven. With the limited mental capacity that we develop here on this earth, we cannot comprehend the beauty and splendor of our heavenly home.

The sea of glass represents tranquility. Not the temporary moments of partial respite we sometimes experience in our worldly life, but a marvelous, never ending, never interrupted, total peace that we cannot imagine at this point and time.

These tribulation saints are experiencing that heavenly bliss as a reward for their unwavering faith and perseverance. The mingling with fire represents the purification of these saints through their faith and trust in the gospel of salvation through the blood of the Lamb. While the church had already been raptured, God still offered his message of mercy through the tribulation witnesses, and it was from them that these individuals heard the message of salvation.

John sees seven angels appear from the Heavenly Temple. These angels, because of their breastplates of gold, and their emergence from the temple, are considered by some scholars to be acting as "priests of God". One of the four beasts that constantly attend the throne of God hands each of them a golden vial, filled to the brim with the wrath of God. *And the temple was filled with smoke from the glory of God and from his power---.* This vision compares with the experience of Moses on the mountaintop when he received the Ten Commandments from God. Remember that while the people did not see what Moses saw, they still saw the smoke and fire on the mountain. While God's presence is never hidden from mankind, there are times when he makes his presence known in a special way. The experience of Moses and the Israelites when God gave the Ten Commandments; the cloud by day and the pillar of fire by night in the wilderness, are examples of this.

I believe this vision is an indication of the very same phenomenon, where God comes to the forefront to personally supervise the culmination of his judgment on satan and sinful man.

CHAPTER 16

1. And I heard a great voice out of the temple saying to the seven angels, go your ways, and pour out the vials of the wrath of God upon the earth.

THE VIALS

Most scholars believe as I do that the great voice coming from the temple is the voice of God himself, instructing the angels to pour out their vials. These judgments are far more terrible than any that have come before. While the previous judgments affected only a certain portion of the earth and its inhabitants, these final judgments are all encompassing. They also come in rapid succession.

2. And the first went, and poured out his vial upon the earth; and there fell a noisome and grievous sore upon the men which had the mark of the beast, and upon them which worshipped his image.

The first angel pours out his vial and every non-believing person on the earth receives loathsome sores. These sores are probably in the form of boils or ulcers of the skin that are incurable and cause tremendous pain. Note that only those who have the mark of the beast are affected which leads me to believe that those who trust and believe in God are not only spared this judgment, but all the rest of the vial judgments. When there is no water, God will quench their thirst. When there is darkness, they will have spiritual sight. When the heat becomes unbearable, they will be cooled by the glory of God.

3. And the second angel poured out his vial upon the sea; and it became as the blood of a dead man: and every living soul died in the sea.
4. And the third angel poured out his vial upon the rivers and fountains of waters; and they became blood.

The second angel pours out his vial and the seas become blood; not a third part as before, but all the seas of the earth. Every living being in the seas dies. This is followed by the third angel pouring out his vial on all fresh water, and it too turns to blood. Imagine the smell. As the sea is the source of much of the world's food, imagine the famine this creates.

5. *And I heard the angel of the waters say, thou art righteous, O Lord, which art, and wast, and shalt be, because thou hast judged thus.*
6. *For they have shed the blood of saints and prophets, and thou hast given them blood to drink; for they are worthy.*
7. *And I heard another out of the altar say, even so, Lord God Almighty, true and righteous are thy judgments.*

John hears an angel proclaiming the just nature of God's actions. The forces of the devil are now forced to drink blood because: *They have shed the blood of the saints and the prophets.*

8. *And the fourth angel poured out his vial upon the sun; and power was given unto him to scorch men with fire.*
9. *And men were scorched with great heat, and blasphemed the name of God, which hath power over these plagues: and they repented not to give him glory.*

The fourth angel pours out his vial and the sun becomes so hot that it literally scorches the men of earth. I know that everyone reading this book has at some time in their lives had severe sunburn. Remember the agony it caused? Picture this about tenfold!

Picture the plight of the earth's inhabitants at this point. They have cancerous sores, are forced to drink blood, and now their skin is scorched. The rivers of blood, the putrid sores, and the scorched flesh combine to produce an unbearable stench. Their reaction is to curse and blaspheme the name of God. In their minds, they probably feel that they are not deserving of such punishment, but in reality, the decision is God's alone. There is no excuse or argument that will stay his hand. Their cursing and blasphemy only serve to amplify the rightness of God's decision.

10. And the fifth angel poured out his vial upon the seat of the beast; and his kingdom was full of darkness; and they gnawed their tongues for pain,
11. And blasphemed the God of Heaven because of their pains and their sores, and repented not of their deeds.

This is a literal physical darkness; the total absence of light. Most of us have never experienced this total absence. The darkness of the darkest night is still only a partial darkness. Those who have experienced total darkness describe it as a frightful sobering experience. Picture the inhabitants of the earth, already in acute physical pain, tormented by the sudden upheaval of their surroundings, suffering from thirst and hunger, now plunged into total darkness. They gnawed their tongues for pain. By this time, sinful man must surely realize that his fate is sealed. It must be remembered that, upon God's promise that every soul be given a chance to respond to the Gospel, not one of these can claim ignorance as an excuse. Every single one will look back and remember a time when he was given the opportunity to accept Christ as savoir and refused him.

12. And the sixth angel poured out his vial upon the great river Euphrates; and the water thereof was dried up, that the way of the kings of the east might be prepared.
13. And I saw three unclean spirits like frogs come out of the mouth of the dragon, and out of the mouth of the beast, and out of the mouth of the false prophet.
14. For they are the spirits of devils, working miracles, which go forth unto the kings of the earth and of the whole world, to gather them to the battle of that great day of God Almighty.

The sixth angel pours out his vial and the great river Euphrates is dried up, providing access to the Kings of the east that they might come to the gathering of forces for the battle of Armageddon, here referred to in verse fourteen as: the battle of the great day of God Almighty.

The three unclean spirits that come one out of the mouth of the dragon, one out of the mouth of the beast, and one out of the mouth of the false prophet, go forth to gather the nations of the earth to the battle.

Having been a senior non-commissioned officer in the U.S. Army in a combat theatre, I am familiar enough with military intelligence and battle plans to know that no nation would send it's armies in to battle against an unknown foe. The first and prime objective in preparing for battle is to obtain as much intelligence about the enemy as possible prior to formulating the final battle plans. While the nations that ally themselves to the antichrist may not know for certain that they are fighting directly against their creator, they must surely be aware that the enemy claims allegiance to God, and that God has already wrought many terrible works of judgment against which they were powerless to resist. The utter futility of their task will cause them to be fanatical in a last ditch effort to attain victory. Their hopes will be dashed to bits when they are defeated by an army of one in the person of Christ Jesus, the King of Kings, and Lord of Lords, as we will see in a later chapter.

15. Behold, I come as a thief. Blessed is he that watcheth, and keepeth his garments, lest he walk naked, and they see his shame.

Here is a warning in the words of Christ himself. The garments he speaks of is the spiritual covering; the faith and knowledge that God will ensure the victory of all believers. Whether the victory comes through death, or the endurance of severe hardships; through sustaining faith in God's promises, the believer can be assured of final triumph.

This particular warning at this particular time would lead one to believe that there are still some believers on the earth, and as this chapter leads up to the great battle of chapter nineteen, it is safe to assume that these saints will be on the earth when that battle occurs.

We will find in later chapters that some of these saints never leave earth but go into the millennial kingdom with Christ.

16. And he gathered them together into a place called in the Hebrew tongue Armageddon.

Aided by the coercion of the three spirits of devils of verse fourteen, satan gathers all the nations of the earth to the field of battle.

17. And the seventh angel poured out his vial into the air; and there came a great voice out of the temple of Heaven, from the throne saying, it is done.
18. And there were voices, and thunderings, and lightnings; and there was a great earthquake such as was not since men were upon the earth, so mighty an earthquake, and so great.
19. And the great city was divided into three parts, and the cities of the nations fell: and great Babylon came in remembrance before God, to give unto her the cup of the wine of the fierceness of his wrath.
20. and every island fled away, and the mountains were not found.
21. And there fell upon men a great hail out of Heaven, every stone about the weight of a talent: and men blasphemed God because of the plague of the hail; for the plague thereof was exceeding great.

As part of the seventh vial we see two last plagues visited on sinful mankind. The first is an earthquake of such magnitude that all the great cities of the earth are destroyed. No earthly convulsion of nature could possibly cause such a catastrophic event. This will come directly from the hand of God.

Special attention is given to great Babylon, the seat of the antichrist, which we will see in later chapters is most probably the city of Rome.

The second plague is equally supernatural; a hailstorm in which every stone is about the weight of a talent. This computes to anywhere between sixty and one hundred pounds! Once again, mankind's reaction is anger and blasphemy against God.

The great voice, coming directly from the throne, in verse seventeen, must surely be the voice of God. His announcement that it is done signals that with the plagues of the seventh vial, his torment of the earthly inhabitants is finished.   With the seven trumpets, then the seven vials, his wrath is now appeased.   From this point on, there will be no more opportunity for repentance.

THE FALL OF BABYLON

The battle of Armageddon follows directly after the seventh vial but the vision of this great battle does not occur until the end of chapter nineteen.   In between the seventh vial and the great battle, God takes a break in the time line to expound on the destruction of Babylon.   He reveals her great sins and her even greater punishments in great detail.

In the following chapters we see two separate narratives of the same story, each told in a slightly different manner.   God did this in his description of creation in the book of Genesis with two separate narratives, and he published four separate narratives of the gospel message in the New Testament.

Chapter seventeen deals with the destruction of the antichrist's system with emphasis on the whore church.   Chapter eighteen parallels chapter seventeen but concentrates on the political and economical nature of the system.

CHAPTER 17

THE WHORE CHURCH

1. And there came one of the seven angels which had the seven vials, and talked with me, saying unto me, come hither; I will shew unto thee the judgment of the great whore that sitteth upon many waters:

It is my belief that the whore represents the apostate "one world church", born of the antichrist, and ministered by the false prophet. An interesting comparison can be made between the "whore", or apostate church, vile and evil, and the "bride", or true church of Christ, pure and chaste.

2. With whom the kings of the earth have committed fornication, and the inhabitants of the earth have been made drunk with the wine of her fornication.

This verse addresses the power and influence that this apostate church will have over the nations of the earth, reminiscent of the position of the Catholic Church during the reformation period of the late fourteen hundreds. During that period there was a bishop in nearly every king's court. He was authorized to collect taxes for the church, he advised the king on political as well as religious matters, and to a great degree, he dictated the religious doctrines of the nation. The office of court bishop was deliciously attractive to those individuals who had no aversion to using the office to amass power, privilege, and wealth in their own name, and many such individuals sought these positions. I believe that the apostate church of the antichrist will follow this same pattern as the evil nature of the society he controls will cause it to naturally develop along these same lines.

3. So he carried me away in the spirit into the wilderness; and I saw a woman sit upon a scarlet coloured beast, full of names of blasphemy, having seven heads and ten horns.

John is carried away in the spirit to the wilderness. Perhaps this wilderness represents the apostate condition of society, wrought by the power of the antichrist and his counterfeit church. Any society lacking the lordship of Christ would, by its nature, be a spiritual wilderness.

I saw a woman sit upon a scarlet beast--. The seven heads and ten horns definitely identify the beast as the antichrist. The woman represents the whore church, and the fact that she is riding the beast represents her power and influence. This also represents the fact that the beast provides her with the mobility, authority, and access to allow her to influence the nations of the earth.

4. And the woman was arrayed in purple and scarlet colour, and decked with gold and precious stones and pearls, having a golden cup in her hand full of abominations and filthiness of her fornication:

The description of the woman indicates the decadence that comes from self aggrandizement. Whenever societies or individuals become self serving, "self" becomes a false idol, or a false god, in disobedience of the first commandment. The goal of attainment becomes the single focus, and nothing moral or physical is allowed to distract the attention from this pursuit.

5. And upon her forehead was a name written, MYSTERY, BABYLON THE GREAT, THE MOTHER OF HARLOTS AND ABOMINATIONS OF THE EARTH.

The name written on her forehead represents the brazenness of her nature. It would seem that she is not only totally satisfied with her position, but she is in fact proud of it. This is reminiscent of the practice of harlots during the height of the Roman Empire, of wearing a label on their foreheads containing their name.

6. And I saw the woman drunken with the blood of the saints, and with the blood of the martyrs of Jesus; and when I saw her I wondered with great admiration.

The "one world church", because of its alliance with the antichrist, will succeed in gaining a religious monopoly. In an effort to alleviate the "holy wars" that keep erupting because of the tensions between major religions, this one world church will attempt to embrace all of these groups at once. There will be no room for basic doctrines particular to any one group, and any tenet that is offensive to any one group will not be permitted. What will emerge is a "mish mash" of "holy rules" that satisfy the masses. It will be a "whatever feels good" religion that recognizes no deity other than the assumed deity of the antichrist and satan.

What I am about to say will probably anger some readers, but I am at least ninety percent certain that most of our major denominations of today will allow themselves to be assimilated into the one world church for the purpose of promoting world peace and harmony. Some may have reservations, but out of convenience, or fear of extinction they too will reluctantly join.

It will be declared criminal to worship "in spirit and in truth" and those who do will pay the price in blood. You may think it heartless of God to allow their deaths, but consider the consequences. They can die, and enter into the Heavenly bliss, or they can stay alive and endure severe hardships for what will seem to be a very long time, and then die anyway. Which would you prefer?

Why then does God not take them all through death? In order for his overall plan to come to complete fruition, he must maintain a core of believers on the earth. This core, however, will not be left to the mercy of the evil ones. This core will enjoy divine protection and strength sufficient to carry them through as long as they maintain their faith in God's promises. The purpose of this core will be to still offer hope to sinful man, through God's offer of redemption.

When I first read verse six, I was astounded that John would say that he admired this woman. How could a man as holy and filled with the love and spirit of God as John was, admire her?   Dr. Strong's concordance gave me the answer.   The Greek word used in the original text was THAUMA, which means to wonder.   This word stems from the root word THEAOMI which means to look closely; to perceive; to behold.   I took this then to mean to behold in wonder.   This then made the passage totally agreeable with my estimate of the character of John.

THE REVIVED ROMAN EMPIRE

7. *And the angel said unto me, wherefore didst thou marvel? I will tell thee the mystery of the woman, and of the beast that carrieth her, which hath the seven heads and ten horns.*

8. *The beast that thou sawest was, and is not; and shall ascend out of the bottomless pit, and go into perdition: and they that dwell on the earth shall wonder, whose names were not written in the book of life from the foundation of the world, when they behold the beast that was, and is not, and yet is.*

The angel begins to explain the vision to John.   The beast that was and is not and yet is represents not just the antichrist but his form of government as well.   His kingdom will be set up much like a carbon copy of the old Roman Empire.   The Roman Empire had a very unique form of government for it's time, that was born in paganism, ruled in tyranny, considered itself to be above all others, and the populace was forced to consider the emperor a deity.

The kingdom of the antichrist will not be a literal revival of the old Roman Empire, but will be so similar that the resemblance will be unmistakable.   This is why the prophetic writings about the end times often identify the kingdom of the antichrist with the Roman Empire thus, the description "Was, is not, yet is".

Another reason for this association is that the seat of the antichrist's government is thought by nearly all Bible scholars to be the city of Rome.   You may be thinking, "How about the association with Babylon?"   The identification with the Roman Empire signifies the physical nature of the antichrist's kingdom, while the identification with Babylon signifies the spiritual nature of his kingdom.   Babylon was perhaps the most apostate kingdom of the Old Testament, and its geographical location coincided with the location of the ancient tower of Babel, where mankind first began to openly rebel, and defy the rule of God.

9. And here is the mind that hath wisdom.   The seven heads are seven mountains, on which the woman sitteth.

In this verse we find a clue that also points favorably to the city of Rome as the seat of government for the antichrist, the mention of seven mountains.   For centuries one of the names for the city of Rome has been "The city of seven hills."

10. And there are seven kings: five are fallen, and one is, and the other is not yet come; and when he cometh, he must continue a short space.

Who are the seven kings?   The text plainly states: five are fallen, one is, and the other is yet to come.   Some scholars believe them to be the Roman Emperors in this order: (1) Caesar Augustus 31BC-14AD, (2) Tiberius 14AD-37AD, (3) Caligula 37AD-41AD, (4) Claudius 41AD-54AD, (5) Nero 54AD-68AD, (6) Vespasian 69AD-79AD, (7) Titus 79AD-81AD, and (8) Domitian 81AD-96AD.   If we count the first five as fallen, (Augustus to Nero) then the one who "is" would be Vespasian.   We know that John was exiled to the island of Patmos by Emperor Domitian who succeeded Titus in 81AD, after his death.   Therefore we can readily see that the "emperor" theory does not fit the description of Five are fallen, one is, and the other is yet to come.   This theory is disproved by the facts.

Another theory, (which I support), is that these kings represent empires that have ruled over the nation of Israel.   The five that are fallen are: (1) Egypt, (2) Assyria, (3) Babylonia, (4) Medo-Persia, and (5) Greece.   Now we come to the one that is.   The Roman Empire controlled nearly the entire known world, including Israel; at the time that John wrote the book of revelation.   The seventh king, the one which is *"not yet come"* is the kingdom that "was; was not; yet is", the kingdom of the antichrist, the revived Roman Empire.   This theory fits perfectly with the rest of the prophesy, as well as the prophesies of the Old Testament.

11. And the beast that was, and is not, even he is the eighth, and is of the seven, and goeth into perdition.

I believe that the beast that is the eighth, and of the seven represents the kingdom of the antichrist in two stages, the first stage being the first three and one half years, the second stage being the last three and one half years. The reason that I separate it this way is that there will be such a marked difference between the two stages, especially where it concerns his relationship to the nation of Israel. These two periods will be so diametrically opposed, that they will literally seem like two totally different governments.

THE TEN KINGS

12. And the ten horns which thou sawest are ten kings, which have received no kingdom as yet; but receive power as kings one hour with the beast.
13. These have one mind, and shall give their power and strength unto the beast.

The ten kings represent a federation of nations that will swear allegiance to the antichrist. Most Bible scholars are in agreement that this federation will be European nations, and at present that seems to be the only possibility. The European Union is already in the embryonic stage of becoming just such a federation. This probability of the formation of a "United States of Europe" should be taken as a dire warning by all those individuals who say in their hearts, "I still have plenty of time." IT IS LATER THAN YOU THINK!

When I consider that these have received no kingdom as yet, it seems that these kings will emerge for the first time near the middle of the tribulation period. They will most probably be puppets, totally subservient to the antichrist, and appointed by him to replace the governments that will be in place at the time. In order for this to happen, these governments must be so weak that they cannot resist the coercion of the antichrist. Just as a side note, the United States must also cease to be a world power and be brought to its knees as both a financial and military power before the antichrist can consolidate his kingdom. Our current trends toward acceptable immorality and financial greed will result in just such a failure if left unchecked. I can see no possibility of these trends being reversed, short of divine intervention and judgment.

The alliance of this federation with the antichrist will occur at some time during the tribulation period, but the exact timing is not divulged. The fact that they receive power one hour with the beast is a fairly ambiguous clue. The only information that can be derived from this clue is that the partnership will be short-lived. The "one hour" could possibly mean the last three and one half years of the tribulation period. There are, however, still some clues to come in the rest of the chapter.

14. These shall make war with the Lamb, and the Lamb shall overcome them; for he is Lord of Lords, and King of Kings: and they that are with him are called, and chosen, and faithful.

The ten kings make war with the Lamb. I believe that this act of making war is not a single battle, but rather their participation in the ongoing conflict between the forces of God, and the devil. This participation will begin with their pact with the antichrist, and end in the battle of Armageddon. Along with all the other nations, they will take part in the antichrist's persecution of all believers, especially the Jews. Throughout history, most European nations have openly voiced a dislike for the Jews, and would need little or no urging to focus on their persecution.

Here is another clue that points to their short term of reign with the antichrist as being near the end of the tribulation period: I believe the phrase: the Lamb shall overcome, alludes to the battle of Armageddon, therefore, their reign has to be shortly before the battle.

The last part of the verse must surely speak of the army of saints that will accompany Christ to this battle.

16. And the ten horns which thou sawest upon the beast, these shall hate the whore, and shall make her desolate and naked, and eat her flesh, and burn her with fire.

17. For God hath put in their hearts to fulfill his will, and to agree, and give their kingdom unto the beast, until the words of God shall be fulfilled.

18. And the woman which thou sawest is that great city, which reigneth over the kings of the earth.

We see a remarkable event happening here. While it seems to be totally out of character, at some point during the latter part of the tribulation, the ten kings will persecute the one world church. This persecution will be severe and intense, and whether they realize it or not, (I suspect they will not), they will actually be acting under God's control. One might ask, "Why does the antichrist not try to intervene?" There is no loyalty among thieves. The one world church, as well as the ten kings, is merely tools to be used by the antichrist to further his ruthless, ambitious goals. God will cause him to compare the usefulness of one against the other, and the antichrist will come to the conclusion that the ten kings are more important to him, and the sacrifice of the world church is just a minor setback.

Here is yet another clue to indicate that the alliance between the ten kings and the antichrist happens during the latter part of the tribulation, as the world church will most probably be active during almost all of the tribulation period, therefore, the persecution by the ten kings must surely come near the end of the tribulation period.

THE SECOND NARRATIVE

Chapter eighteen is basically a strong indictment against the entire system of the antichrist, with emphasis on the physical and economical injustices and excesses of the wicked kingdom.

CHAPTER 18

1. And after these things I saw another angel come down from Heaven, having great power, and the earth was lightened with his glory.

2. And he cried mightily with a strong voice, saying, Babylon the great is fallen, is fallen, and is become the habitation of devils, and the hold of every foul spirit, and a cage of every unclean and hateful bird.

3. For all nations have drunk of the wine of her fornication, and the kings of the earth have committed fornication with her, and the merchants of the earth are waxed rich through the abundance of her delicacies.

The angelic announcement that Babylon is fallen is both prophetic and historical. Historical in the sense that the city of the antichrist's government was destroyed at the pouring out of the seventh vial; prophetic, alluding to the coming battle of Armageddon when all power shall be taken from the antichrist and the false prophet, and they shall be thrown into the lake of fire for eternity.

The phrase: is become the habitation of devils, and the hold of every foul spirit--- could be speaking of the current condition of total apostasy, or the miserable condition of the city after it's physical destruction. It will be totally unfit for any habitation except for devils and foul spirits in either case.

In verse three, we see the extent of the economic power of this evil system. Due to the nature of this apostate society, fairness will be considered a weakness, and unethical practices will be the rule of the day. These merchants will curry favor with the antichrist in order to amass great personal wealth and status, and will feel smug and secure under his protection.

4. And I heard another voice from Heaven, saying, come out of her, my people, that ye be not partakers of her sins, and that ye receive not of her plagues.

I believe this verse to be a universal warning to all who read the book of revelations to abandon the pursuit of worldly property, power, and prestige that have become false gods to so many, and to separate ourselves from the world. We need not wait until the tribulation period to do this.

Isaiah 1:18-20 *Come now and let us reason together, saith the Lord, though your sins be as scarlet, they shall be white as snow; though they be red like crimson, they shall be as wool. If ye be willing and obedient, ye shall eat the good of the land: but if ye refuse and rebel, ye shall be devoured with the sword; for the mouth of the Lord hath spoken it.*

II Corinthians 6:17-18 *Wherefore come out from among them, and be ye separate, saith the Lord, and touch not the unclean thing; and I will receive you, and will be a Father unto you, and ye shall be my sons and daughters, saith the Lord Almighty.*

The scripture makes it very clear that we are to have no intimate relationships with worldly pursuits. The practice of placing worldly pursuits before our service to God has been around since Adam and Eve, and many are engrossed in it. It is remarkably easy to just follow the crowd, but the excuse that "everybody is doing it" will have no effect on God's ear, now, or on judgment day.

5. For her sins have reached unto Heaven, and God hath remembered her iniquities.

For her sins have reached up to Heaven--- This is not to imply that there is some kind of delay before God receives knowledge of sin, for we know that absolutely nothing ever escapes his immediate scrutiny. What this passage means is that her sins have become so great in frequency and magnitude that all Heaven takes note.

And God remembered her iniquities. Once again, this does not imply that God forgot them for a while, rather, this is a way of saying that her hour of reckoning has arrived. Her sins have become so great that they demand God's immediate attention.

6. Reward her even as she rewarded you, and double unto her according to her works: in the cup which she hath filled fill to her double.

7. How much she hath glorified herself, and lived deliciously, so much torment and sorrow give her: for she sayeth in her heart, I sit a queen, and am no widow, and shall see no sorrow.

8. Therefore shall her plagues come in one day, death, and mourning, and famine; and she shall be utterly burned with fire: for strong is the Lord God who judgeth her.

Her judgment will be swift; her judgment will be severe. Verse seven speaks of her complete arrogance. She stands boldly in the face of God and says in essence: "you cannot harm me." She seems totally ignorant of the power of God. Verse eight speaks of swift, terrible judgment. For strong is the Lord God who judgeth her. God's omnipotent power can be seen and felt in the splendor of creation and in the wonderful order of the universe. For any being to assume the ability to defy this power with even the minutest degree of success is sheer madness. There is no power on earth or in Heaven but that which is granted by God.

THE KINGS MOURN

9. And the kings of the earth, who have committed fornication and lived deliciously with her, shall bewail her, and lament for her, when they shall see the smoke of her burning,

10. Standing afar off for the fear of her torment, saying, alas, alas, that great city Babylon, that mighty city! For in one hour is thy judgment come.

The kings of the earth who have benefited from their alliance with the antichrist now disassociate themselves and stand afar off, for the destruction of that great city, the seat of the evil empire, is almost too awesome to behold. Their re-action is not one of repentance, but of sorrow for themselves. Their benefactor, from whom they received their power, is helpless before their eyes. He no doubt promised them protection, and that together they would defeat the Lamb. They must now stand in amazement and watch the destruction of the seat of his kingdom, as well as their own hopes for the future. *For in one hour is thy judgment come.* I believe that this means: now is the hour of your judgment.

THE MERCHANTS MOURN

11. And the merchants of the earth shall weep and mourn over her; for no man buyeth their merchandise any more:

12. The merchandise of gold, and silver, and precious stones, and of pearls, and fine linen, and purple, and silk, and scarlet, and all thyine wood, and all manner vessels of ivory, and all manner vessels of the most precious wood, and brass, and iron, and marble,

13. And cinnamon, and odours, and ointments, and frankincense, and wine, and oil, and fine flour, and wheat, and beasts, and sheep, and horses, and chariots, and slaves, and souls of men.

14. And the fruits that thy soul lusted after are departed from thee, and all things which were dainty and goodly are departed from thee, and thou shalt find them no more at all.

15. The merchants of these things, which were made rich by her, shalt stand afar off for fear of her torment, weeping and wailing,

16. And saying, alas, alas, that great city, that was clothed in fine linen, and purple, and scarlet, and decked with gold, and precious stones and pearls!

The merchants who grew rich through the corrupt economic system; the same system that was based on the mark of the beast; the system that denied commerce to all who remained faithful to God; must now suffer the same agony that the kings endured. They will look upon all the worldly treasure that they have amassed, and will come to the realization that all their wealth cannot do a single thing toward easing the physical and spiritual condition of poverty that they now find themselves to be in. How they must tremble in anticipation of their coming judgment before God.

THE SHIPMASTERS MOURN

17. For in one hour so great riches is come to nought. And every shipmaster, and all the company in ships, and sailors, and as many as trade by sea, stood afar off,
18. And cried when they saw the smoke of her burning, saying, what city is like unto this great city!
19. And they cast dust on their heads, and cried, weeping and wailing, saying, alas, alas, that great city, wherein were made rich all that had ships in the sea, by reason of her costliness! For in one hour is she made desolate.

Try to imagine a situation where all the worlds' commerce was stopped for a period of only 48 hours. Can you visualize the chaos that would arise?

As a small example, the stock market crash in America in the nineteen thirties created such turmoil that ex-millionaires were committing suicide. Multiply that turmoil by at least a thousand fold and you can visualize what the economic conditions on the earth will be like when the kingdom of the antichrist is destroyed.

You will recall that the seas were turned to blood, and all the creatures in them died. While sailors are for the most part, a hearty lot, I doubt that any would dare venture out on the "bloody seas". Due to sheer panic among the seafaring men, all maritime commerce will stop. A major portion of the world's goods is transported on ships across the oceans of the earth. When this shipping ceases, there will be total pandemonium. Just as the kings and merchants did, the shipmasters and sailors will stare in unbelief and fear at the destruction that is taking place before their very eyes. Their ships will be motionless; their future in deep peril.

CELEBRATION OF THE SAINTS

20. Rejoice over her, thou Heaven, and ye holy apostles and prophets; for God hath avenged you on her.

In direct contrast to the anguish felt by the worldly society of the antichrist, all Heaven can now celebrate. With the total destruction of the unholy city, God has exacted vengeance on the system of the antichrist in the name of the martyred saints. Going back to chapter six, verse ten, *how long, O Lord, holy and true, dost thou not judge and avenge our blood on them that dwell on the earth?* Their desire is now come to fulfillment. Their waiting is over. While the world had lived in luxurious excesses; the saints had to endure ridicule, persecution, torture, even death; and now the tables are turned. There is great rejoicing and exaltation throughout all Heaven; on earth, total despair.

THE FINALITY OF THE DESTRUCTION

21. And a mighty angel took up a stone like a great millstone, and cast it into the sea, saying, thus with violence shall that great city Babylon be thrown down, and shall be found no more at all.

22. And the voice of harpers, and musicians, and of pipers, and trumpeters, shall be heard no more in thee; and no craftsman of whatsoever craft he be, shall be found any more in thee; and the sound of a millstone shall be found no more at all in thee.

23. And the light of a candle shall shine no more at all in thee, and the voice of the bridegroom and of the bride shall be heard no more at all in thee: for thy merchants were the great men of the earth; for by thy sorceries were all nations deceived.

24. And in her was found the blood of the prophets, and of saints, and of all that were slain upon the earth.

The act of the angel throwing a great millstone into the sea is symbolic of the totality and finality of the destruction. All of the normal every day activities within the city will cease. The great evil city will become a wasteland forever. This giant millstone, once it disappears below the waves, will never be seen again. There will be no physical evidence that it ever existed. This will be the condition of that great evil city. It will be so completely destroyed, that an onlooker would never know that it once existed.

CHAPTER 19

THE CELEBRATION

1. And after this I heard a great voice of much people in heaven. Saying, Alleluia, salvation, and glory, and honour, and power, unto the Lord our God:

2. For true and righteous are his judgments: for he hath judged the great whore, which did corrupt the earth with her fornication, and hath avenged the blood of his servants at her hand.

3. And again they said, Alleluia. And her smoke rose up for ever and ever.

4. And the four and twenty elders and the four beasts fell down and worshipped God that sat on the throne, saying, A-men; Alleluia.

5. And a voice came out of the throne, saying, praise our God, all ye his servants and ye that fear him, both small; and great.

The destruction of the great evil city is now a reality. The physical destruction is representative of the accompanying destruction of the apostate system that began at the tower of Babel. This system was propagated by satan through all the ages, and he is now powerless to resist its defeat. Her smoke rose up for ever and ever. This is symbolic of the finality of her destruction. All Heaven has ample reason to rejoice, and does so wholeheartedly. The power that satan formerly exercised over the earth is now broken.

THE MARRIAGE SUPPER

6. And I heard as it were the voice of a great multitude, and as the voice of many waters, and as the voice of mighty thunderings, saying, alleluia: for the Lord omnipotent reigneth.

7. Let us be glad and rejoice, and give honour to him: for the marriage of the Lamb is come, and his wife hath made herself ready.
8. And to her was granted that she should be arrayed in fine linen, clean and white: for the fine linen is the righteousness of saints.
9. And he saith unto me, write, blessed are they which are called unto the marriage supper of the Lamb. And he sayeth unto me, these are the true sayings of God.

In verse six, we see all Heaven rejoicing and praising God for the victory that is not physically complete as yet, but it's imminence is so assured that there can be no doubt. The kingdom of the antichrist is in physical and spiritual shambles, and the only act left undone is the destruction of the army of satan at Armageddon, which is about to come. The system of the antichrist is destroyed, and his doom is assured. *The Lord God omnipotent reigneth.* There are three characteristics of God that are uniquely his own. These are: OMNIPRESENCE, OMNIPOTENCE, and OMNISCIENCE.

We determined earlier that omnipresence means the ability to be in all places at the same time. Omnipotence which is mentioned here means that God has sole proprietorship over all power in Heaven and on earth. Omniscience is the ability to have all knowledge of the past, present, and future.

As to omnipresence, I once saw a wall plaque that read: "Jesus, the unseen listener to every conversation; the unseen spectator to every deed; the unseen guest at every meal." What a sobering thought, that every word we speak, every thought of our mind is recorded in Heaven. It is equally sobering that every act we perform is recorded as though our entire life were on video tape.

As to omnipotence, there is absolutely no power in Heaven or on earth that did not come directly from God. Even satan can produce no power of his own, but can only utilize the limited powers that God has afforded him.

As to omniscience, God has absolute knowledge of every minute detail of the past, present, and future. Just as a comparison, an avid student of history, totally focused, and spending his entire life exclusively on this pursuit, could perhaps amass the knowledge of one one hundredth of one percent of all the details of the past, while

God knows one hundred percent, as well as one hundred percent of the future!

In verses seven and eight, we read about the marriage of the Lamb. The Lamb of course is Christ; the bride is the raptured church.

I believe that most born again members of the church fail to fully appreciate their unique position as the bride of Christ. The patriarchs of the old Testament are not included in the bride, nor are the prophets, nor the tribulation saints. While they are the blessed that are called to the wedding supper in verse nine, they are invited guests and not part of the bride. To some, this may seem that God is being unfair in that he seems to favor one group over another.

I was deeply concerned as to how to explain this apparent disparity, so I called my pastor. In the midst of our conversation it came to me that God's grace was only offered during the church age. Those not included in the bride received forgiveness, but I received a full pardon. There is a definite difference. Let me give you two examples.

Moses was a great man of God and served him well, but because he became upset with God on one occasion, He was not allowed to enter the Promised Land. God escorted Moses to a mountain top where he could look upon the Promised Land, but God told him that because of his sin, he would not be allowed to lead the people there, and Joshua was chosen in his stead. We know that Moses went to Heaven, as he was seen along with the prophet Elijah and the glorified Christ on the mount of transfiguration in chapter nine of the gospel of Mark.

This leads us to my second example. The prophet Elijah was another great man of God. He was a faithful servant who stopped the rain for three and a half years with a simple prayer; he restored the rain with another prayer; he defeated and killed the four hundred and fifty prophets of Baal, single handedly through the power of God, and a short time later he was hiding in a cave, having a pity party. God came to him in the cave and told him to arise, and anoint a new king over Israel, and also to anoint a man named Elisha as a prophet in his stead.

In both of these cases, God discharged each man from his service and replaced him with another. We know that he forgave them after their punishment as they were both seen with the glorified Christ on the mount of transfiguration. They were, however made to pay for their sins.

The born again believers, whose sins are covered by the blood of the Lamb of God, stand sinless before the throne. Not that we have never sinned, for we have, I would dare say much more so than Moses or Elijah, but our punishment was borne by another, the savior, Jesus Christ. The payment has already been made in full, and we have no sin debt obligation.

The raptured church is Christ's true love, for which he gave his life, through terrible pain and anguish; therefore it is accorded the title: "the Bride of the Lamb".

Verse seven states: *and his wife hath made herself ready.* The preparation of a bride for the wedding ceremony has always been a very special process. This process is nearly as memorable to the bride as the ceremony itself. Individually, each born again believer has a very special remembrance of the time when they surrendered to the pleadings of the Holy Ghost. Collectively, as the church, we look back fondly on the pathway we have trod. With fondness, we remember both the good and the bad. The good times we enjoyed in sweet fellowship with each other in our Lord; the bad times when we discovered just how much strength we drew from each other through the power and presence of Jehovah God. There need be no unpleasant memories.

Verse eight explains that the fine linen is symbolic of the righteousness of the saints. This righteousness is not of ourselves, but the righteousness that is only applied through the blood of the Lamb of God. It has always amazed me that God can take a heart that is black as coal, wash it in blood that is crimson red, and it comes out white as snow!

Before I was born again, I made feeble attempts at various times in my life to make myself better morally. I experienced varying degrees of temporary success, and at times, I became proud of my accomplishments along these lines. It was not until I received the plain old gospel message in all its power that I came to realize just how tainted my successes must seem to God. I came to the same realization that Paul did in Romans chapter seven, verse twenty four when he wrote: *O wretched man that I am---*. While these self improvements served me in good stead in my daily living, I came to discover that they were worthless to die by. The only way to erase my failures was to cover them in the blood of God's sacrificial Lamb, Jesus the Christ, my savior!

THE WEDDING GUESTS

19:9 Blessed are they which are called unto the marriage supper of the Lamb. We have already mentioned three groups who will not be included in the bride: the Old Testament patriarchs, the Old Testament prophets, and the tribulation saints. There is actually a fourth group, the Old Testament disciples of God. We could actually fit those, the Old Testament patriarchs, and the Old Testament prophets into one category called the Old Testament saints.

Those Old Testament saints who believed in, and submitted to, the sovereignty of God, were chastised whenever they sinned, and then forgiven. The annual sacrifice sufficed to cancel out their condemnation for their sins.

The tribulation saints who were alive prior to the rapture had the opportunity to accept Christ and did not; therefore, not including them in the bride seems justified. Those who are born during the tribulation will not reach the age of accountability, will be taken in their innocence, and will share in the invitation of the other tribulation saints.

All of these groups will be the "blessed" who are called to the wedding supper.

10. And I fell at his feet to worship him. And he said unto me, see thou do it not: I am thy fellow servant, and of thy brethren that have the testimony of Jesus: worship God: for the testimony of Jesus is the spirit of prophesy.

In this verse, John falls prey to a temptation that has entangled many a saint. The message of the angel has such a positive effect on him that he attempts to worship the messenger. There is a very fine line between admiration and adoration (worship). It is highly acceptable to admire one who is in the service of God, and ministering tirelessly to all whom they come in contact with. There is no sin in being vocal about that admiration. The problem comes when we ascribe godly qualities to that person. For instance, when a godly saint lays hands on someone who is sick and they are healed, it seems natural to give that saint credit for the miracle, when in actuality; they are merely a conduit for the miracle working power of God.

As a member of his flock, you should have a very special love for your pastor. If you don't love your pastor, you are in the wrong church; but if you will follow him anywhere he transfers to, no matter what effect it has on the house of God, that is worship. You are placing your relationship with him above your relationship with God. I have seen so many Christians do this, and it saddens me every time I see it.

KING OF KINGS AND LORD OF LORDS

11. And I saw heaven opened, and behold a white horse; and he that sat upon him was called Faithful and True, and in righteousness he doth judge and make war.

12. His eyes were as a flame of fire, and on his head were many crowns; and he had a name written, that no man knew, but he himself.

13. And he was clothed with a vesture dipped in blood: and his name is called the Word of God.

14. And the armies which were in heaven followed him upon white horses, clothed in fine linen, white and clean.

15. And out of his mouth goeth a sharp sword, that with it he should smite the nations: and he shall rule them with a rod of iron: and he treadeth the winepress of the fierceness and wrath of Almighty God.

16. And he hath on his vesture and on his thigh a name written, KING OF KINGS, AND LORD OF LORDS.

Here we see Christ come down from Heaven on a white horse. We will see in later verses that the armies of Heaven come with him, also on white horses. I don't know if there will be literal horses, or if the reference is symbolic. I tend to favor the latter.

106

In ancient warfare, the horse cavalry was the elite fighting force. They were highly mobile, could strike rapidly, and quite often were able to defeat a much larger conventional force. The vision of horses could be symbolic of this unique elite standing. The fact that all the horses are white stands for the purity of this army of God, for all the saints, who make up the majority of this army, have washed their robes in the blood of the Lamb, and stand clad in garments whiter than snow. What a magnificent sight for John to behold, as they approach on their white horses, clad in their white robes, with Christ at the fore.

Christ is described as faithful and true. Christ, in his first coming, never took a single step, uttered a single word, commandeered a single moment in his own behalf, but was totally focused upon the will of the Father, which was the redemption and sanctification of mankind. His steadfastness and devotion and sacrifice earned for him the right to return as judge and executioner.

In righteousness he doth judge and make war. It is absolutely fitting that Christ should be the one who completes God's master plan. Remember, it was he alone, because of his life on earth of sinlessness, total self denial, and sacrifice, which uniquely qualified him to open the seven seals and begin the period of judgment. There have been many attempts by the secular media of late to humanize Christ. These are concoctions of the devil; but sadly, many people today are eager to accept these lies as factual, even though they are only conjecture, without one iota of proof. If just once, Christ exhibited any form of human weakness, then he would not qualify as the Lamb of God, without spot or blemish.

19:11 THE SHEEP/GOAT JUDGMENT

One of the first acts of Christ at the beginning of the millennium will be the judgment of the nations. While it is a widely accepted theory that only whole nations will be judged, this theory is not accepted by all, including myself.

While the text of Mathew chapter twenty five says that all nations shall be gathered, it is my belief that each individual of each nation will be judged separately.

Let us examine what "thus saith the Lord."

MAT 25:31-34 *When the son of man shall come in his glory, and all the holy angels with him, Then shall he sit upon the throne of his glory. And before him shall be gathered all nations and he shall separate them one from another, as a shepherd separates his sheep from the goats. And he shall set the sheep on his right hand, but the goats on the left. Then shall the King say unto them on his right hand, come, ye blessed of my Father, inherit the kingdom prepared for you from the foundation of the world.* Now let us go down in the same chapter to verse forty one: *Then shall he say unto them on the left hand, depart from me, ye cursed, into everlasting fire, prepared for the devil and his angels.*

I can find no reference in any of the text that would lead me to believe that entire nations will be judged collectively. The phrase "before him shall be **gathered** all nations" merely indicates to me that no one shall be exempt.

There are two clues in the beginning of the passages from Mathew that definitely point to this judgment being at the beginning of the millennium. First, the only time in the scripture that Christ and "all the angels" come down to earth in one group is at the beginning of the millennium. Secondly, he speaks of sitting on the throne of his glory. This must surely mean the throne of David, in the city of Jerusalem, the site of Christ's millennial reign.

I believe that those who will be summoned to this judgment will be those, both lost, and saved, who survive the tribulation. The saved will enter the kingdom; the lost will be cast into the lake of fire.

Going back to the theory that this will be a judgment of nations rather than individuals, I submit that it would be out of character for God to cast whole nations into the lake of fire. God holds each individual wholly responsible for their own sins, thus sin is punished individually, not collectively. We will also see in later text that these nations still maintain their autonomy as they are gathered by satan at the end of the millennium to do battle with Christ. While I do believe that God judges nations, especially in regard to his promise to Abraham, (I will bless them that bless you, and curse them that curse you), this punishment consists of removal of blessings and replacing them with curses, and it is an ongoing judgment, not a one time event.

His eyes were as a flame of fire--- This is symbolic of the warrior Christ. There is a certain resolution that can be seen in the eyes of a great warrior. Nearly all the great warriors of the past have been described as having that look, and Christ has now taken on the role of a mighty man of war.

On his head were many crowns--- These crowns are symbolic of all the kingdoms of the earth which are about to come under his dominion. While Christ has always been spiritually King of Kings, and Lord of Lords, he will now take up this position physically, and rule upon the earth in person.

He had a name written which no man knew--- In verse thirteen we see that his name is called "The Word of God". In the gospel of John, chapter one, verse fourteen, God says the Word was made flesh and dwelt among us. This Word represents the wisdom of God which no man can know except the Son of God and the Holy Ghost, exclusive members of the triune Godhead of Father, Son, and Holy Ghost.

And he was clothed with a vesture dipped in blood--- this blood is symbolic of the judgment of Christ's enemies. The penalty for sin must be totally implemented. There can be no peace on earth or in Heaven until sin has been dealt with in its entirety.

In verse fourteen we see the armies of Heaven following Christ. Note that the word armies is plural. I believe that Heaven is emptied for this event. I believe these armies are the angels, the Old Testament Saints, and the New Testament saints all together. They all have a right to share in the final victory.

In verse fifteen we see the actual description of his righteous judgment. While the armies of Heaven follow him, I believe they have no part in the actual destruction except that of spectators. The sharp sword that goes out of his mouth is symbolic of the power of his spoken word. He need only speak and it shall come to pass.

In reference to the treading of the winepress of the fierceness and wrath of Almighty God, let us go back to the book of Isaiah, chapter sixty three, and verse three: *I have trodden the winepress alone; and of the people there was none with me: for I will tread them in mine anger, and trample them in my fury; and their blood shall be sprinkled on my garments, and I will stain all my raiment.* There is a definite parallel between this verse and verse fifteen, and also a reference to the vesture dipped in blood in verse thirteen. It is most amazing how the book of revelations and the Old Testament prophets correlate. The wording of this passage from the book of Isaiah is one of the main reasons that I believe that Christ performs this final judgment by himself. Also, he alone is worthy to perform it, and with all the power and authority of God at his disposal, he has no need for any assistance.

In verse sixteen we see that Christ's title of "King of Kings, and Lord of Lords" is written on his vesture and on his thigh. It is my belief that this was written by the hand of God himself, to notify all who see it that all the power and might of Heaven are designated in that title, and are at his disposal.

THE SECOND FEAST

17. And I saw an angel standing in the sun; and he cried with a loud voice, saying to all the fowls that fly in the midst of heaven, come and gather yourselves together unto the supper of the great God.

18. That ye may eat the flesh of kings, and the flesh of captains, and the flesh of mighty men, and the flesh of horses, and of them that sit on them, and the flesh of all men, both free and bond, Both small and great.

19. And I saw the beast, and the kings of the earth, and their armies, gathered together to make war against him that sat on the horse, and against his army.

In direct contrast to the wedding supper of the Lamb, we see here another feast in which man is the main course instead of an invited guest. Every person on the face of this earth will attend one of these feasts. Each and every person reading this book who is not saved is faced this moment with three choices. There are no alternatives. (1)You can accept Christ as your savior now, (2) or you can wait and go through the terrible anguish of the tribulation period, and possibly accept him; a decision for which you may have to die hideously for, (3) or you may just ignore the whole gospel message and one day be the entrée at the feast of the fowls. It is my fervent prayer that you have already opted for the first choice, but if you haven't yet, please consider it now. Make no mistake, a failure to choose will absolutely, positively qualify you for the third choice!

Most people picture the battle of Armageddon as a mighty battle with swords clashing, and flags flying, some even consider it to be world war three. I submit that it will be far less dramatic than most people visualize. As we have already read in previous text, Christ needs only to speak death and destruction and it will take place. The armies of the devil will have absolutely no chance to even begin to make war. It will be a totally one sided conflict; Christ will speak, and they will die. Note in verse seventeen that the feast of the buzzards will be all inclusive. No one will escape this destruction. In verse twenty it says that the birds will be filled with their flesh. I can just picture all the birds of the earth walking around because they are so full that they can not fly!

20. And the beast was taken, and with him the false prophet that wrought miracles before him, with which he deceived them that had received the mark of the beast, and them that worshipped his image. These both were cast alive into a lake of fire burning with brimstone.
21. And the remnant were slain with the sword of him that sat upon the horse, which sword proceeded out of his mouth: and all the fowls were filled with their flesh.

In verse twenty we see a remarkable event in that the antichrist and the false prophet are taken in judgment before satan is. In this verse it says that they are cast alive into a lake of fire burning with brimstone. I can imagine them appealing to satan for the protection that he has promised them, and he being powerless to assist them.

One should not get the wrong impression from the words cast alive into a lake of fire burning with brimstone. One might easily assume that they will die in the fire and their bodies be consumed to ashes. This is not the case. All those who are cast into the lake of fire, will be cast in alive, will remain alive, and never, throughout all eternity, receive even the smallest respite from the searing pain. In a trillion years, this pain will not diminish one iota!

CHAPTER 20

THE MILLINEAL REIGN OF CHRIST

1. And I saw an angel come down from heaven, having the key of the bottomless pit and a great chain in his hand.

2. And he laid hold on the dragon, that old serpent, which is the devil, and satan, and bound him a thousand years.

3. And cast him into the bottomless pit, and shut him up, and set a seal upon him, that he should deceive the nations no more, till the thousand years should be fulfilled: and after that he must be loosed a little season.

The first step in setting up the millennial kingdom, is to bind satan in the bottomless pit. His influence will be removed from mankind for the next thousand years, after which he will be loosed for a short time.

4. And I saw thrones, and they sat upon them, and judgment was given unto them: and I saw the souls of them that were beheaded for the witness of Jesus, and for the word of God, and which had not worshipped the beast, neither his image, neither had received his mark upon their foreheads, or in their hands; and they lived and reigned with Christ a thousand years.

5. But the rest of the dead lived not again until the thousand years were finished. This is the first resurrection.

6. Blessed and holy is he that hath part in the first resurrection: on such the second death hath no power, but they shall be priests of God and of Christ, and shall reign with him a thousand years.

Verses four and five speak of the first resurrection. Verse six reads: *Blessed and holy is he that hath part in the first resurrection: on such the second death hath no power,* --- We will explain the second death in the section on the great white throne judgment. Who is included in this first resurrection? Every saint that dies up until the end of the millennium. I believe this resurrection will happen in stages.

We already know about the resurrection that will take place at the rapture. I Thes 4:16-17 *For the Lord himself shall descend from Heaven with a shout, with the voice of the archangel and with the trumpet of God: and the dead in Christ shall rise first: then we which are alive and remain shall be caught up together with them in the clouds, to meet the Lord in the air: and so shall we ever be with the Lord.* This I would consider to be the first stage. In verse four we see a description of the tribulation martyrs who have been resurrected. I would consider this the second stage. Now we come to those mortals who survived the tribulation and went on to the millennium.

In the period of one thousand years, they all will surely die. Perhaps these will enter into an immortal state immediately upon death, or there will be a third stage at the end of the millennium, in either case, they will also be resurrected.

I find it most remarkable that the book of revelations does not describe the conditions of everyday life during this reign, but the book of Isaiah describes it wonderfully. Some scholars believe the description in Isaiah to be so "far fetched" that it must be symbolic, but I wholeheartedly disagree. I not only believe the description to be absolutely literal, but also that it brings mankind back to the relationship between man and nature that Adam and Eve enjoyed in the Garden of Eden before the original sin.

I once heard a radio evangelist telling of a man who argued with him that "you couldn't possibly make a Lion eat straw." The evangelist replied: "If you will make a lion, I will make him eat straw." Impossible with man; child's play for God!

FROM THE BOOK OF ISAIAH

2:4 And he shall judge among the nations and shall rebuke many people; and they shall beat their swords into plowshares, and their spears into pruning hooks: nation shall not lift up sword against nation, neither shall they learn war any more.

11:1-9 And there shall come forth a rod out of the stem of Jesse, and a branch shall grow out of his roots; and the spirit of the Lord shall rest upon him, the spirit of wisdom and understanding, the spirit of counsel and might, the spirit of knowledge and of the fear of the Lord. And shall make him of quick understanding in the fear of the Lord; and he shall not judge after the sight of his eyes, neither reprove after the hearing of his ears: But with righteousness shall he judge the poor. And reprove with equity for the meek of the earth: and he shall smite the earth: with the rod of his mouth, and with the breath of his lips shall he slay the wicked. And righteousness shall be the girdle of his loins, and faithfulness the girdle of his reins. The wolf also shall dwell with the lamb, and the leopard shall lie down with the kid; and the calf and the young lion and the fatling together; and a little child shall lead them. And the cow and the bear shall feed; their young ones shall lie down together; and the lion shall eat straw with the ox. And the suckling child shall play on the hole of the asp, and the weaned child shall put his hand on the cockatrice' den. They shall not hurt nor destroy in all my holy mountain; for the earth shall be full of the knowledge of the Lord, as the waters cover the sea.

I have heard the opinion that this description in the book of Isaiah applies to the eternal kingdom that will come after judgment day, but a careful examination of the text disproves that theory.

The phrase: with the breath of his lips shall he slay the wicked leaves that theory in the dust! There will be no wicked in the eternal kingdom, therefore, this must be a description of the millennial reign.

There are also three references to children in the description of Isaiah: (1) and a little child shall lead them.

(2) And the suckling child shall play on the hole of the asp. (3) And the weaned child shall put his hand on the cockatrice den. There will be no children in eternity; there will be no aging; there will be no measurement of time; therefore, this must speak of the millennium.

It is readily apparent from the above description that life in the millennium will be quite different from our life as we live it today. There is, however, a dark side. This will not be utopia. Mankind will still have freedom of choice and even though they are physically cognizant of Christ's rule, many will still deny his lordship.

As we read later on, satan is released from the bottomless pit at the end of the millennium and will gather an army to fight against Christ. This army will most certainly be made up totally of non-believers, born during the millennium, so the conflict between good and evil will still exist during the thousand years., as well as man's freedom of choice, otherwise satan could gather no army.

The full scope of the millennial kingdom is hard to describe, and to understand. There will be several classes of people on the earth and life will probably be quite different than most people will picture it. First, Christ will dwell and reign physically on the earth. Not the "Son of Man" as he often identified himself during his first advent on the earth, but the glorified "Son of God". Not the benevolent, forgiving, compassionate Jesus with whom we are most familiar, but the stern, immovable, Christ, King of Kings, and Lord of Lords, who will rule with a rod of iron, judging without favor or slackness. I believe his first act will be to judge among the nations and rebuke many people, to slay the wicked with the breath of his lips, as stated in the text. He will re-institute true worship and fellowship among all living beings.

Then there will be the saints from Heaven; All those who have been martyred for their beliefs, as well as those who have passed away before the rapture, and all those who are taken in the rapture. These will all be in their glorified bodies, in their white robes, and those who were martyred will rule with Christ.

The next group is somewhat controversial, as many scholars deny their existence, but I submit that in order for the millennial kingdom to close as it is recorded in verses eight, nine, and ten, There has to be a rather large number of mortal men and women who are all believers, and survive the tribulation, to enter into the millennial kingdom. Now here is the reason I believe that such a group must exist: When satan is loosed from the bottomless pit at the end of the millennium, he gathers a second army against Christ. Where does this army come from? We know that his first army was totally destroyed at the battle of Armageddon, therefore, this army must consist of individuals who were born during the millennium. Due to the fact that all of the saints who enter the millennium via Heaven are in an immortal state, genderless, and incapable of childbearing, there must also be mortal men and women in order to produce the offspring who will become this second army of the devil.

7. And when the thousand years were expired, satan shall be loosed out of his prison,

8. And shall go out to deceive the nations which are in the four quarters of the earth, Gog and Magog, to gather them together to battle: the number of whom is as the sand of the sea.

9. And they went up on the breadth of the earth and compassed the camp of the saints about, and the beloved city; and fire came down from God out of heaven, and devoured them.

10. And the devil that deceived them was cast into the lake of fire and brimstone, where the beast and the false profit are, and shall be tormented day and night for ever and ever.

Various attempts have been made to identify Gog and Magog as used in verse eight as specific nations. While these names are given in the Old Testament to indicate specific nations, I believe that these names, as used here, are merely symbolic of all the heathen nations due to the use of the phrase "the nations which are in the four quarters of the earth".

Just as the first army was totally destroyed, so will be this one. As we see in verse eight, this army will be great in number. They will surround the city of Jerusalem, the seat of Christ's government and fire will come down from God out of Heaven and totally devour this army. The devil will then be cast into the lake of fire where the antichrist and the false prophet have already been for a thousand years, and there they will remain for eternity.

I am adamant about the fact that I have absolutely no desire to share their fate, nor will I, as I have accepted the truth in God's word; I believe in salvation through the shed blood of his only begotten son; I am a humble partaker of the free gift of His Amazing Grace. I am continually troubled whenever I encounter those hapless individuals who deny the gift, or even it's very existence, as I know beyond a shadow of doubt that they will spend eternity in the lake of fire along with the devil and his henchmen!

You may say "I don't believe it." Are you so willing to take that chance? Is there not a strong possibility that God really exists? Is it not equally as strong a possibility that the only way to Heaven is by believing in the gospel message of the Bible? The gospel (good news) about salvation by believing in the substitutionary death of the Son of God on the cross of Calvary, through which the believer receives total forgiveness for sin?

Doubt if you must, but as for me, I will live and die secure in the knowledge that my eternal soul has been redeemed; and that one day, body and soul will be joined together in Heavenly bliss. BELIEVE IT!

THE GREAT WHITE THRONE JUDGMENT

11. And I saw a great white throne, and him that sat on it, from whose face the earth and the heaven fled away; and there was found no place for them.

We now come to the end of our world as we know it. The countenance of him that sat on it (the great white throne) will be so awesome that the earth and heaven will flee away from the face of him. Not Heaven with a capital H but heaven with the lower case; not the abode of God and the angels, but the atmosphere around the earth.

It is commonly believed that this judgment takes place somewhere in limbo rather than in Heaven. It cannot take place on the earth as it is now gone. It is my belief that this is a special setting and not the throne of God. I also believe that Christ is the one sitting in judgment on the throne. John 5:22 *for the Father judgeth no man, but has committed all judgment unto the Son.*

12. And I saw the dead, small and great, stand before God; and the books were opened: and another book was opened, which was the book of life: and the dead were judged out of those things which were written in the books, according to their works.
13. And the sea gave up the dead which were in it; and death and hell delivered up the dead which were in them: and they were judged every man according to their works.
14. And death and hell were cast into the lake of fire. This is the second death.
15. And whosoever was not found written in the book of life was cast into the lake of fire.

These four verses record the actual process of the judgment. All of the dead who were not taken in the first resurrection will take part in this judgment.

These are the rest of the dead noted in verse five. By the same token, not one saint will take part in this second resurrection, as their eternity has already been secured.

All of the unsaved dead will be there. Not one sinner will escape. Even those who were cremated will be there as it will be a simple task for God to reassemble their ashes on that day.

Note that the term death and hell are used twice in the text. Death is the temporary abode of the body; hell the temporary home of the soul. Body and soul will be reunited at this second resurrection, just as the body and soul of the saint was at the first, with one major difference. The saint received a new immortal body; the damned will attend "come as you are". Their body will stay in the wretched condition that it was in when it entered the grave.

The text describes several books that will be present, opened, and used at this judgment. There is one voluminous set of books which contain a record of every deed, every thought, every act, of every person there. Then there will be another book, called the "Lamb's Book of Life." In it are all the names of those who have accepted Christ as their savior. The purpose for this book being at this judgment is to show that the participant's names are not found there, and to cause them to reflect on what could have been. I do not believe that these deserving sinners will be cast into the lake of fire for the deeds that are recorded in the books of deeds, as Christ has already paid the price for all the sins of mankind, but these records will be used to show that they "sinned and came short of the glory of God", and were therefore in need of a savior. Then the book of life will be searched in vain for their name, and when it is not found, they will be indicted for and found guilty of **not accepting the savior** that God provided in their behalf. This will be the sin that will send them into the lake of fire for an eternity. John 3:18 He *that believeth on him is not condemned: but he that believeth* *not is condemned already, because he hath not believed in the name of the only begotten son of God.*

Most people would picture the crowd that stands before the throne as a motley group of unsavory thugs and hoodlums, but I submit that there will be a lot of good people there. There will even be many who call themselves Christians.

These are they whom Christ spoke of in Mat 7:21-23: *Not every one that saith unto me Lord, Lord, shall enter the kingdom of Heaven; but he that doeth the will of my Father which is in Heaven. Many shall say to me in that day, Lord, Lord, have we not prophesied in thy name? And in thy name have cast out devils? And in thy name done many wonderful works? And then will I profess unto them, I never knew you: depart from me, ye that work iniquity.*

When Christ says "in that day" he is talking about a specific event in time, and this must surely mean the great white throne judgment. I can think of no other.

We can readily see from the description of their works that these are people who actively participated in the Christian lifestyle, and probably were members in good standing of a dynamic local church. They probably attended services regularly, tithed faithfully, and participated in all sorts of programs, but they had really not accepted Christ as their savior in their heart of hearts. How terribly, utterly, sad when their charade is exposed on that day. Some of these will probably consider themselves to have had a salvation experience in which they truly believed, but if their motive was anything other than true repentance; their experience could not possibly have been genuine. Sadly, they will spend eternity in the lake of fire.

There will be another group of good upstanding non-believers who lived their life to the best of their abilities by the humanist moral code, which closely parallels the Christian way. A good humanist is a wonderful person to know; to deal with; to have living next door. They are for the most part, upstanding citizens in their community. Their only mistake will have been turning a deaf ear to the truth in God's eternal word. These too will spend eternity in the lake of fire.

When these hapless individuals are judged solely according to their works, and they will be, every single one will have at least one sin among their many good works.

Romans 3:23 *For all have sinned and come short of the glory of God.* Romans 3:20 *Therefore, by the deeds of the law, there shall no flesh be justified in his sight—*
I would venture to say that in most cases, the good works will vastly outnumber the sins. Is it then fair, if one does ten thousand good works and only one sin, that he be punished for that one sin? Let us examine the situation. In order for God to justify in his own heart, any punishment at all, he must be totally, eternally fair. Would it be fair to let one sin slide by and yet punish others? I think not. While mankind, by his nature, is capable of such behavior, God is not! God must punish each and every sin or none at all.
You may say "what about the sins of the saints? After all, they had sin in their lives too." Their sins were not simply passed over, but God the Father allowed Christ, the only begotten son to bear this punishment in it's entirety in the stead of any who would believe in that sacrificial substitution. It's that simple folks. The opportunity is open to all. John 3:16 says *whosever believeth in him*; that doesn't leave anybody out. Christ is an equal opportunity savior!

THE SECOND DEATH
There is documented evidence that strongly suggests the existence of the "soul" of man.
There was a secular movie that was shown some time back, (I think it was in the sixties), narrated by Orson Welles, called "Beyond and Back". I distinctly remember a portion of that movie which told of an experiment that was performed on dying individuals, as well as dying animals. Their death beds were placed on sensitive scales, and at the moment of death, there was an instantaneous slight weight loss that occurred in each individual, that did not occur in any of the animals. To this day, nothing in science can account for this phenomenon. This was proof positive that there was a difference in the death of a person, and an animal.

There was also a sequence in the movie that related a story of nuns in a Catholic hospital, who saw a wispy cloud they described as "like a vapor" rise from a dying body and disappear upward through the ceiling. This occurrence was considered so unique, that it was recorded in the hospital records. It was commonly believed by all who were present at this event that the vapor was the soul of the departed.

While these occurrences do not definitely prove the existence of the soul, one must admit that they strongly suggest it!

God's word says the soul of the non-believer, upon their death, will exist in torment until the great white throne judgment when body and soul will be rejoined to be cast into the lake of fire. He identifies this as the second death.

To fully realize the extreme magnitude of this second death, one must picture himself in the place of the non-believer.

The non-believer has some small measure of hope, seasoned with doubt. He does not have the same certainty about his future that is common to all saints. First, he has a hope that if there really is a God, (he doesn't know for sure), he hopes that he (God) will overlook his sins in light of his good deeds, (Wrong on both counts). Or secondly, he hopes there is no God, and that when he dies, his body will remain in the grave in a state of non-consciousness forever. (Wrong again).

I believe that the majority of people who call themselves non-believers, are actually not. I have never met a person who could state with any kind of self assurance that God does not exist. If I should ever meet one, I will be sure to ask him: "On what evidence do you base that statement?"

Most non-believers actually feel in the recesses of their minds, that there is a slight possibility that God really exists. While they outwardly deny him, they are secretly hoping desperately that they are right. Meanwhile, they breath his air, they eat his food, they are warmed by his sunshine; in short, they are sustained and pleasured by his creation. I believe the deepest torment of all in their eternity in the lake of fire will be the realization that they were wrong, and the fault for their plight is totally their own. The truth that they denied will be constantly upon their minds. They will long desperately for an opportunity to renegotiate with God, but to no avail; their doom is sealed! Once they stand before the white throne, there is no more chance for renegotiating.

Actually, renegotiate is not a good choice of words, as the requirements that God has set for entry into eternal bliss are not negotiable. His requirements are clear, concise, and forever settled in his holy word. Compliance is not optional or negotiable, but man is forever testing God's resolve in this area. Those who do are in for a rude awakening at the great white throne.

CHAPTER 21

A NEW HEAVEN AND A NEW EARTH

1.   And I saw a new heaven and a new earth: for the first heaven and the first earth were passed away, and there was no more sea.

There are two distinctive schools of thought about this passage. The first, which I hold to, is that there will be a literal destruction of the entire universe; the earth and it's atmosphere will cease to exist, and be replaced by the new heaven and the new earth that John saw. This is the belief of nearly all fundamental Christians.

The second school of thought is more liberal, in that it contradicts the literal translation, by suggesting that the earth will be cleansed, or regenerated, by God, and returned to use.   I fail to see how these thinkers can justify the last part of this passage when God says: "the first heaven and the first earth were passed away."   No amount of liberal translation can change the fact that God says they are gone.

This belief in a cleaned up earth probably stems from the fact that if the earth and it's atmosphere were suddenly removed, the universe would go into a cataclysmic upheaval, and that would not fit their concept of life as usual, but on a higher plane.   They are actually placing natural limits on God.   God is supernatural; he has no limits!   He is capable of making anything happen, whenever he wants it to happen, any way he wants it to happen.

In reality, if one takes the Bible literally, (as I do) it speaks specifically of just such a cataclysmic event.   There are several references to this occurrence in the Old Testament prophets, as well as in the New Testament.   I have selected one from each.

ISA 54:4 *And all the hosts of heaven shall be dissolved, and the heavens shall be rolled together as a scroll.*

REV 6:13-14 *And the stars of heaven fell unto the earth, even as a fig tree casteth her untimely figs, when she is shaken of a mighty wind. And the heaven departed as a scroll when it is rolled together; and every mountain and island were moved out of their places.*

These two verses sound to me like a little more than life as usual on a higher plane. I suspect that these descriptions picture the total destruction of the universe as we know it.

THE GREAT CITY; NEW JERUSALEM

2. And I John saw the holy city, New Jerusalem, coming down from God out of heaven, prepared as a bride adorned for her husband.
3. And I heard a great voice out of heaven, saying, behold, the tabernacle of God is with men, and he will dwell with them, and they shall be his people, and God himself shall be with them, and be their God.

John sees the great city, New Jerusalem, the eternal abode of the Believers in Christ, come down from Heaven. This city will be described in detail in verses ten through twenty five.

Verse three describes a very remarkable event. I use the word remarkable as I feel that some if not most readers will not fully grasp the magnitude of this verse. Behold, the tabernacle of God is with men, and he will dwell with them, and they shall be his people, and God himself shall be with them and be their God.

Mankind has now come full circle. The intimate personal fellowship that God shared with Adam and Eve in the Garden of Eden as described in Genesis, chapter two, and the first part of chapter three is now restored; the fellowship that was destroyed by the original sin. God, in his perfection, could not abide with sin, therefore he had no choice but to terminate that fellowship until the cancer of sin was permanently removed from mankind. The plague is now eradicated; and holy harmony descends upon the relationship between creator and creation. Oh the bliss of an eternal moment, shared with Jehovah God!

4. And God shall wipe away all tears from their eyes; and there shall be no more death, neither sorrow, nor crying, neither shall there be any more pain, for the former things are passed away.

5. And he that sat upon the throne said, behold, I make all things new. And he said unto me, write: for these words are true and faithful.

6. And he said unto me, it is done, I am Alpha and Omega, the beginning and the end. I will give unto him that is athirst of the fountain of the water of life freely.

7. He that overcometh shall inherit all things; and I will be his God, and he shall be my son.

8. But the fearful, and unbelieving, and the abominable, and murderers, and whoremongers, and sorcerers, and idolaters, and all liars, shall have their part in the lake which burneth with fire and brimstone: which is the second death.

Just as a loving father attends lovingly and sacrificially to all the needs of his family, so God will meet all of our needs. In eternity, we will lack for nothing. There will even be no need to ask; as God will anticipate and fulfill our every desire as it arises. By the same token, our desires will never be selfish or sinful, but will be totally in keeping with our new lifestyle of complete harmony and holiness.

In verse five God says: Behold, I make all things new. Our first thought when reading this is probably about physical things; the new earth, the new heaven, the great city, but a much more important aspect of this phrase is the totally new relationship between all creation, whose author and creator is God. This new relationship will be totally harmonious and eternally orchestrated by God.

Not only will we have an intimate relationship with God, but also with each other. There will be no cliques in eternity. What we now label as "human nature" will be non-existent there.

In verses six through eight, God summarizes his judgment of mankind. It is finalized, never to be modified or reversed. When God says: I am alpha and omega, the beginning and the end, he is clearly stating his sovereignty over all creation. His absolute power and authority are unquestionable; his actions and edicts irreversible.

JOHN SEES THE CITY

9. And there came unto me one of the seven angels which had the seven vials full of the seven last plagues, and talked with me, saying, come hither, I will shew thee the bride, the Lamb's wife.

10. And he carried me away in the spirit to a great and high mountain, and shewed me that great city, the holy Jerusalem, descending out of heaven from God.

11. Having the glory of God: and her light was like unto a stone most precious, even like a jasper stone, clear as crystal;

12. And had a wall great and high, and had twelve gates, and at the gates twelve angels and names written thereon, which are the names of the twelve tribes of the children of Israel:

13. On the east three gates; on the north three gates; on the south three gates, and on the west three gates.

14. And the wall of the city had twelve foundations, and in them the names of the twelve apostles of the Lamb.

15. And he that talked with me had a golden reed to measure the city, and the gates thereof, and the wall thereof.

16. And the city lieth foursquare, and the length is as large as the breadth: and he measured the city with the reed, twelve thousand furlongs. The length and the breadth and the heighth of it are equal

17. And he measured the wall thereof, an hundred and forty and four cubits, according to the measure of a man, that is, of the angel.

18. And the building of the wall of it was of jasper: and the city was pure gold like unto clear glass.

19. And the foundations of the wall of the city were garnished with all manner of precious stones. The first foundation was jasper; the second, sapphire; the third, a chalcedony; the fourth, an emerald;

20. The fifth, sardonyx; the sixth sardius; the seventh, chrysolyte; the eighth, beryl; the ninth, a topaz; the tenth, chrysopasus; the eleventh, a jacinth; the twelfth, an amethyst.

21. And the twelve gates were twelve pearls; every several gate was of one pearl: and the street of the city was pure gold as it were transparent glass.

22. And I saw no temple therein: for the Lord God Almighty and the Lamb are the temple of it.

23. And the city had no need of the sun, neither of the moon to shine in it: for the glory of God did lighten it, and the Lamb is the light thereof.

24. And the nations of them which are saved shall walk in the light of it: and the kings of the earth do bring their glory and honor into it.

25. And the gates of it shall not be shut at all by day: for there shall be no night there.

26. And they shall bring the glory and honour of the nations into it.

27. And there shall in no wise enter into it any thing that defileth, neither whatsoever worketh abomination, or maketh a lie: but they which are written in the Lamb's book of life.

The great city is described in great detail; so much so that one can easily picture it in their mind. The picture one gets, however, is so much of a departure from our normal expectations that it seems like something from a science fiction movie, but because of the precise description, one can only come to the conclusion that this description is exactly what it will look like. While mankind sometimes has a tendency to mislead or exaggerate, God, by his nature, cannot, nor will not.

I imagine most of you reading this book have heard the expression "diamonds are forever". The use of precious stones in building this city is suggestive of its eternal nature. Gems never tarnish nor decay. It will never have need for repair. It will remain in the same state of glory and splendor for eternity. As I said before, God will supply it's every need.

The dimensions of this city are totally awesome. Nothing man has ever made comes close to its size or glory. Its shape is in the pattern of the walled cities of John's day with one major exception. There will be none of the accouterments of defense; no towers, no turrets, no drawbridges at the gates. There will be no need for these things as all our enemies have been vanquished forever, and God will be our protector.

There is no mention of a roof over the city, nor is there any need. The city will be covered and encircled by the glory of God. There will be nothing unpleasant there. All conditions will be exactly to our liking; discomfort will never arise.

While there are gates, there are no windows. Our attention will be forever directed inward, completely focused on our relationship with our creator and our fellow saints.

There will be no privacy, nor need for such. In this life I often have moments when I desire solitude, away from all outside influences and personal contacts, but in eternity I will welcome with great joy the constant companionship of my creator and my fellow saints.

While Christ said in John 14:2 *In my Father's house are many mansions: if it were not so, I would have told you.* I believe that to picture my mansion as some great palatial abode in the pattern of today, would be in error. While I have not a single clue as to what it will be like, I know that my needs, wants and desires, will be totally different in this new life and this mansion will meet the ultimate requirements of the new "me".

First off, as I wrote previously I will have no desire for seclusion, so this mansion must be open to all association. Another reason for this openness is the fact that I will have no need for protection from the elements as there will be no elements, save the glory of God, which were it denied me for even an instant, by an enclosure, I would be most miserable. Summoning all of my cognitive powers, I cannot begin to comprehend a vision of this mansion, but I do know, upon God's promise, that it will be the ultimate abode.

THE FOUNDATION

21:14   This verse describes the city's foundation as being in twelve sections. As this city is square, there must be three sections on each side, most probably one under each of the twelve gates. On these sections are engraved the names of the twelve apostles of Christ personally sent by him to establish the concepts of unified worship, and evangelism, the two main functions of the church which he created. Some scholars believe that because these names are written on the foundation of the great city that this signifies that they were the foundation of the church. To credit the founding of the church to mere mortals is to deny its holiness. While their ministries were the actual beginning of the church, we know from the scripture that Christ himself is the cornerstone and true foundation

THE MEASUREMENT OF THE CITY

21:15-17   The angel who is escorting John measures the city with a reed of gold.   Its dimensions are astounding: fifteen hundred miles square and fifteen hundred miles high.   That computes to three trillion, three hundred and seventy five million cubic miles of space!   There will definitely be room for all who will believe!

THE MATERIALS OF THE CITY

21:18-21   We have already determined that the precious stones of the walls were chosen for their eternal nature; and doubters will probably say that these gemstones do not exist in sufficient quantities throughout the entire universe; and they would probably be right.   BUT, as it was God who created those that exist at present, would it be such a problem for him to create more?   I think not, for I trust his immeasurable power.

THE ABSENCE OF A TEMPLE

21-22   There will be no need for a temple as the presence of God and the Lamb will permeate every corner of the holy city.   There will be one eternal service there.   I may one day stand between Isaiah and Paul as we sing "How Great Thou Art!"

THE PRESENCE OF THE GENTILES

21:24-26   At first reading of these verses, one might get the impression that there will be whole nations living outside the city and that believers from these nations could come and go at will because of the eternally open gates.   It is my belief that this is not the case at all.   In fact, I do not believe there is anyone outside the Holy City.   Every being alive at the onset of eternity has been qualified for permanent residency in the holy city, as all others who were not qualified have been cast into the lake of fire.   Why then would any of them be living on the outside?   I believe, due to the fact that the word "nations" is used, that these three verses represent the fact that gentiles will now physically be able to enter the Holy of Holies. Under the old Jewish law, gentiles were not allowed in any part of the temple; the Jew on the street was allowed in the common court, but not in the holy place which was reserved for only the priests; and only the high priest could enter the Holy of Holies, and that only once a year to offer the sin offering for the nation.

Since the crucifixion of Christ, all believers have been able to spiritually enter the Holy of Holies, as represented by the tearing of the curtain on crucifixion day, but now, in our new glorified bodies, we are not only able to physically enter there but to remain for eternity. The great city has now become our gigantic Holy of Holies because of the eternal presence of the Shekinah Glory of God, the person of God, and the person of the Son, Christ the king.

It is my belief that the eternally open gates signify the permanence of the security of God's eternal kingdom of which we are a part. The enemy is forever vanquished and we enter into that promised eternal rest.

THE PURITY OF THE CITY

21:27 All sin has been eradicated by the destruction of the sinful non-believers in the lake of fire, and all the inhabitants of the holy city have been transformed into their new immortal bodies, and cleansed of their sinful fleshly nature. Every inhabitant is there because they made a free choice to accept God's amazing grace, the gift of a loving Father to an undeserving child. Now that they have chosen the love and generosity of God, I believe that he has taken away their capacity to even consider sin, therefore there is no possibility of sin erupting there.

CHAPTER 22

THE INTERIOR OF THE CITY

1. And he shewed me a pure river of water of life, clear as crystal, proceeding out of the throne of God and of the Lamb.
2. In the midst of the street of it, and on either side of the river, was there the tree of life, which bare twelve manner of fruits, and yielded her fruit every month: and the leaves of the tree were for the healing of the nations.
3. And there will be no more curse: but the throne of God and of the Lamb shall be in it; and his servants shall serve him:
4. And they shall see his face; and his name shall be in their foreheads.
5. And there shall be no night there; and they need no candle, neither light of the sun; for the Lord giveth them light: and they shall reign for ever and ever.

There is very little description of the interior of this great city, however these verses do mention some very important things that will be there. First and foremost, there will be the throne of God and of the lamb; the river of the water of life; and the tree of life. As we have said previously, God will now dwell with man; or to put it in a more proper perspective, man will now dwell with God.

This brings up some very interesting questions, for which I have no answer.

Will there be any more need for the place we now call Heaven?

Will Heaven and all the heavenly hosts become part of the holy city? Will the holy city actually rest upon the new earth or will it be suspended somewhere in the cosmos?

As I pondered all these questions, I became so frustrated that I even considered abandoning this writing, as I felt totally inadequate for the task. I prayerfully sought the answers from God, but as I prayed, I made the mistake that many of us make in our prayer life; I prayed with a preconceived notion that I MUST have the answers. Eventually, God penetrated my stubbornness with the answer "wait and see". Just as with a surprise birthday gift, the anticipation heightens the enjoyment of the moment; so let us experience together, the anticipation of receiving the answers as we enter that eternal city.

Concerning the river of the water of life and the tree of life, the scripture does not specify whether we, in our immortal bodies will have need of physical nourishment or not. Some scholars point to the last meeting of Christ with his apostles in Luke chapter twenty four as evidence that we will. The scripture states that when Christ appeared among them he asked: "Have ye here any meat?" whereupon they gave him a piece of broiled fish and a honeycomb, and he did eat. These scholars state that as he was most probably in his glorified heavenly body, that this is evidence that we will need physical food. I feel that whether we will or not is irrelevant. What is relevant is the fact that God has provided for our sustenance, whether it shall be both physical and spiritual, or spiritual only. The water of life and the tree of life signify this.

A likely possibility is that the water of life represents our spiritual sustenance, while the tree of life represents the physical, but that is only my supposition. What I do know of a certainty is that all our needs will be met.

Verses three, four, and five deal with our new relationship with our creator; a relationship so superb, so wonderful, so intimate that the adjectives contained in our earthly language can scarcely describe its intensity. We will serve him in love and adoration; we will stand unafraid in his presence and look upon his face; we will bear his name proudly on our foreheads as a glaring testimony of our willing submission to his sovereignty. He will embrace us; he will comfort us; he will surround us with his eternal glory. As I ponder these thoughts, the words of a popular hymn come to mind: "Oh I want to see him, look upon his face. There to sing forever of his saving grace, on the streets of glory, let me lift my voice; cares all past home at last; ever to rejoice."

GOD'S ASSURANCE OF TRUTH

6. And he said unto me, these sayings are faithful and true: and the Lord God of the holy prophets sent his angel to shew unto his servants the things which must shortly be done.

God reassures us that this is not a fairy tale! As he states in chapter one verse one, he now reiterates the validity of the visions that John has seen. I fail to see where anyone after reading the book of revelations can merely cast it aside as totally untrue; or totally unimportant; or totally irrelevant to their life. At the very least, it must cause them to fearfully consider their relationship and responsibilities to God.

7. Behold I come quickly; blessed is he that keepeth the sayings of the prophesy of this book.

In verse seven, God also reminds the reader of the blessing promised in chapter one, verse three. I must remind the reader that this blessing is contingent on keeping the sayings of the prophesy of this book.

MISGUIDED WORSHIP

8. And I John saw these things, and heard them, and when I had heard and seen, I fell down to worship before the feet of the angel which shewed me these things.
9. Then saith he unto me, see thou do it not, for I am thy fellow servant, and of thy brethren the prophets, and of them which keep the sayings of this book; worship God.

John here makes the same mistake that he made once before, in being so enthralled with the message that he tries to worship the messenger. Note that the angel, instead of accepting the praise, warns John against it.

This is a temptation that is very useful to satan because it works so well. When I hear a Christian say: "My favorite preacher is---", I pray that they are not worshipping the messenger more than the message. Some preachers thrive on this adoration, and we have seen this become the downfall of some televangelists. We have also seen whole congregations who started out innocently, but succumbed to the selfish, worldly, desires of cult leadership, I.e. Jim Jones and David Koresh as examples.

THE TIME IS AT HAND

10. And he saith unto me seal not the sayings of the prophesy of this book: for the time is at hand.

John is reminded of the urgency of the need to publish this information that he has so wonderfully received. As opposed to keeping it privately, he is told to go out and share it with the world; the reason being: for the time is at hand.

HE THAT IS---

11. He that is unjust, let him be unjust still; and he which is filthy, let him be filthy still; and he that is righteous, let him be righteous still; and he that is holy, let him be holy still.

I daresay that no one would be so foolish as to suggest that this verse applies to the present time. If it did, the conversion of a sinner would go against the word of God, and this concept would contradict the gospel message. Therefore, this verse must apply to some time in the future. I submit that it will apply only when God witnesses the last conversion of a sinner. Due to his foreknowledge of all things; realizing that there will be no more conversions; he will withdraw his offer of grace.

As of that very moment, and forever after, every person's fate is eternally sealed. At what point in time this will occur, only God knows.

NOW IS THE TIME OF SALVATION!

12. And, behold, I come quickly; and my reward is with me, to give every man according as his work shall be.

13. I am Alpha and Omega, the beginning and the end, the first and the last.

14. Blessed are they that do his commandments, that they may have right to the tree of life, and may enter in to the gates of the city.

15. For without are dogs, and sorcerers, and whoremongers, and murderers, and idolaters, and whosoever loveth and maketh a lie.

16. I Jesus have sent mine angel to testify unto you these things in the churches. I am the root and the offspring of David, and the bright and morning star.

17. And the Spirit, and the bride say, come, and let him that heareth say, come, and let him that is athirst come. And whosoever will, let him take the water of life freely.

18. For I testify unto every man that heareth the words of the prophesy of this book, if any man shall add unto these things, God shall add unto him the plagues that are written in this book:

19 And if any man shall take away from the words of the book of this prophesy, God shall take away his part out of the book of life, and out of the holy city, and from the things which are written in this book.

20. He which testifieth these things saith, surely I come quickly. Amen. Even so. Come Lord Jesus.

21. The grace of our Lord Jesus be with you all. Amen.

Up to this point in this chapter, John has been mostly in the company of one or more of the angels. We now come to a point at the end of the book where either Christ is speaking directly to John, or else John is prophesying in the name of Christ. In either case, the message should be taken by the reader as coming directly from the Lord Jesus Christ.

In verse twelve and again in verse twenty we see the phrase I come quickly. Many people have misunderstood this to mean "I am coming soon" which is not the case. I am certain that what he means here is that his coming judgment will come upon us as a "thief in the night"; suddenly without prior warning; and rapidly unfolding. He may come this instant, or not for a hundred years. I will say this however as to the timing; it would seem that his patience must be wearing very thin!

To misinterpret this to mean "I am coming soon" is to fall into a snare of the devil in that one would think this was written a very long time ago, and he did not come soon, as he said, so the whole thing may just be a fantasy.

That is exactly what satan would like you to believe! Sooner or later, I have not a clue, but I know that he will come!

I have lived my whole life since I was born again in October, 1981, in keen anticipation of savoring that blessed moment when Christ shall come to take me home. Whether I am resurrected from the utter darkness of an earthly grave, or am among those who are "alive and remain", I know beyond a shadow of a doubt that I will on that day come face to face with my savior, Jesus Christ, and that he will welcome me with open arms as the father welcomed the prodigal son.

I can say that with perfect certainty because I know that God is real, that the Bible is his divinely inspired word, and that I have placed my trust in the substitutionary death of Christ on the cross of Calvary, as payment in full for all my sins. I am joyfully looking forward to standing in his presence. It is my earnest prayer that I will meet you there!

APPENDIX

After reading this book, I am sure that some readers may have unanswered questions. My purpose in including this segment in the book is to answer the most common of these.

Without a doubt the foremost question on the reader's mind is: **'When will these things happen?"**

Super market tabloids, self proclaimed seers and prophets, and secular psychics have been erroneously predicting the date for centuries. Like the village people in the story of the boy who cried "wolf", our senses have become deadened to the warnings by their repeated speculations. Every time another falsely predicted date passes, we lose a little more consciousness of the serious nature with which we should consider the coming events. This insensitivity plays right into the devil's hands. Mankind's priority for the present should be preparation, not speculation. I want the reader to know beyond a shadow of doubt, regardless of how many times we have been fooled by satan's misinformation, **GOD'S JUDGMENT WILL COME, AT THE TIME OF HIS CHOOSING!** Even Jesus, when queried by his apostles said "only my Father knows."

If I were to venture a guess (ONLY a guess, NOT a prediction) I would say almost surely in this century; probably within fifty years; more probably within ten years. I expect it could happen any moment.

I base this estimate on several observations. First, on the exponential increase in the depravity of mankind. I must admit that as a sixty nine year old minister of the gospel, my views are somewhat jaded by secular standards, (for which I make no apology), but you, the reader, must admit that morality is definitely on the decline. Entertainment stars, sports figures, politicians, and even judges can commit grave sin, and receive the forgiveness and even adulation of the public. There seems to be a sudden explosion of acceptable immorality. So far, man's efforts to stem the tide have been tantamount to attempting to stop a charging elephant with a slingshot. If man cannot reverse the trend, (he seems to exhibit neither the ability nor the desire to do so), then God must, of necessity intervene. If I was not consciously aware of God's impending judgment, I would have serious doubts about the old adage "crime does not pay".

Secondly, I feel the time is near for the formation of one world government. There is already a world court, although at present it has very limited powers; there are however many in positions of authority who would like to see these powers increased immensely. The collective conscience of mankind today is leaning more and more toward the concept of "my world" rather than "my nation". This concept is unheard of heretofore in history.

There are even some in our own federal government today who advocate turning over certain areas of our governance to the United Nations. These would make world socialism the order of the day, thus playing directly into the hands of the antichrist. While these are just a minority at present, what is alarming is that they are a GROWING minority!

Thirdly, the passionate attempt and partial success of the ungodly to erase God from our culture. In my lifetime I have seen secular mankind go from appreciation of God, to toleration of God, to attempted obliteration of God, all this in a few short years.

As I read the past history of earth, and draw on my own sixty plus years of observation, I see a growing explosion of open hatred toward God and his people, especially the nation of Israel, the apple of his eye.

HOW LONG CAN GOD'S PATIENCE ENDURE?

Why is there such an elaborate, drawn out, chain of events? Why doesn't God just pick a date and say: "O.K., that's it, bad guys go to hell, good guys go to heaven?"

The answer to this question is very complex, but if we take it step by step, we will readily see his reasoning and purpose.

There are millions of people in this world today who recognize no moral authority higher than the conscience of man. They see no visible proof of the existence of God.

There are also many who believe in the possible existence of God, but reject the Biblical accounts. They see him as some wispy ethereal being floating around in the cosmos. They recognize no responsibility to him, nor can they define him, nor do they have any desire to. How does mankind come to be in this situation?

When God made man, he allowed him the freedom to live in whatever manner he chose, without any divine intervention. This was done so that man could be a free agent rather than a programmed robot. In this way, man's relationship to God would be by choice rather than compulsion. One can readily see where a relationship of free choice would be much more satisfying to both God and man than one that is programmed, and without feeling. Because of that freedom, man was capable of rejecting a relationship with God.

While Adam enjoyed an intimate relationship with God, he apparently did not place enough value on that relationship to prevent him from committing the original sin. Because Adam chose to disobey God by bringing sin into the relationship, God modified the relationship by removing himself from the presence of mankind because he could not abide with sin. God's act of removing himself physically from the relationship was actually an act of mercy, in that if he were to continue the relationship as before the original sin, he would have to destroy Adam because of that sin.

While God maintained his distance physically, he still communicated with mankind through selected prophets and patriarchs, and here is where the lack of scientific proof of his existence comes in. Information that is received through a second party is scientifically classified as hearsay, and not to be considered fact unless contact can be made directly with the originator for verification. Hearsay is not binding and can be rejected or accepted at will. God's communication came through these selected men in three ways; the spoken word, the written word, and miracles that were said to be brought about by the power of God, but their explanation was also hearsay in that the observers were told second hand by the selected men that the power of God was responsible. No one other than those who believed by faith, actually saw God involved in these events.

After the birth, life, death, and resurrection of our savior, Jesus Christ, the situation changed somewhat, but God still remained separated from mankind.   While he still selected individuals to communicate through, He sent his Holy Spirit to be his primary agent between himself and man.   While the existence of the Holy Spirit is very real to the believer, he is not readily recognizable to the non-believer.   His gentle pleading to the unbeliever can be easily overpowered by the lusts of the flesh.

In summary, from the time when Adam was banished from the garden, until the beginning of the tribulation, the only evidence of God's existence has been, and will be, hearsay only, in the minds of secular mankind.

Now here is a dilemma.   Because of the distance between God and man, there will be millions at the beginning of the tribulation period who will be "doubting Thomases".   They will be neutral in their consideration of his existence, but would believe if they could only see some proof.

Second Peter 3:9 states that God is *"not willing that any should perish, but that all should come to repentance"*.   In order for these doubting Thomases to repent and turn to God, he extends his mercy once again by gradually revealing himself through this elaborate chain of events just prior to his final judgment.   If he did not do this, many would otherwise perish.

How will I know when the things spoken of in the book begin?

This is without a doubt, the easiest question of all to answer.   A vast majority of Bible scholars agree that it will begin with a monumental event we call the "rapture of the saints", as described in the fourth chapter of I Thessalonians:

13. *But I would not have you to be ignorant, brethren, concerning them which are asleep, that ye sorrow not, even as others which have no hope.*

14. *For if we believe that Jesus died and rose again, even so them also which sleep in Jesus will God bring with him.*

15. *For this we say unto you by the word of the Lord, that we which are alive and remain unto the coming of the Lord shall not prevent them which are asleep.*

16. *For the Lord himself shall descend from heaven with a shout, with the voice of the archangel, and with the trump of God, and the dead in Christ shall rise first;*

17. *Then we which are alive and remain shall be caught up together with them in the clouds, to meet the Lord in the air, and so shall we ever be with the Lord.*

Graves will open up, dead bodies will rise up and millions of the living will follow behind, only to be transformed into heavenly beings, body and soul reunited at the feet of the savior, all in a nano-instant of time. Curiosity overwhelms me when I consider the reaction of those who will be left behind. I have absolutely no inkling as to how the world will try to explain this event, but I do know that many will still not believe in the biblical account.

Immediately following this "rapture" the antichrist will assume his position and the seven year period of his reign will begin.

Some of the explanations I have heard or read about in the past do not coincide with your book. What am I to believe?

One of the most amazing miracles of God's word is the ability of a particular passage to mean one thing to one person, and something else to another. What makes it unique is the fact that the individual interpretation may be correct in both cases depending on the circumstances of the individuals.

I claim no privileged knowledge of God's word. What I have done in this book is record my own interpretation of the events as I perceive they will happen. If I have caused you, the reader, to seriously consider the importance and the enormity of these events, even in disagreement, then I have achieved my goal of bringing them to the forefront of your consciousness.

If I can cause just one non-believer to accept God's free gift of salvation by trusting in the substitutionary death of his only begotten son as payment in full for their sins, then the expense and effort I have put forth will not have been in vain.

Whether we agree or disagree on the particulars, there are several points in the book of revelations where even the most abstract of interpretations come into agreement.

1. Life as we know it will someday come to an end. This end will be wrought by, and at the direction of, Almighty God.

2. At the time of that ending, there will be catastrophic judgment on ALL those who chose not to believe, and act upon, God's instructions.

3. The existence of mankind is not finite, but is eternal. By his own choices and actions, each will secure a place of either eternal torment or eternal bliss. There is no middle ground.

4. Every mortal person, whether living or dead, must one day face divine examination. **ARE YOU READY?**

After reading your book, I want to accept Christ as my savior; how do I do that?

It is actually so simple that even an old country boy like me could do it. (I did.) It requires no special ceremony, no secret rites; it is merely a matter of personal conviction.

First you must realize that while your conduct so far may have seemed acceptable to you and those around you, it has fallen far short of what God has said it should be.

Romans 3;23 *For all have sinned and come short of the glory of God.* I am speaking now to the unbeliever, one who is not really sure that God exists.

If there is no afterlife, then you have nothing to worry about, but, if there is, and God is in control of it, (I for one am absolutely certain on both points), then who do you think is responsible for defining the requirements? If you have the slightest inkling that God exists then your relationship to him should be of utmost

142

concern. When God says in his word that your conduct just doesn't measure up, it doesn't measure up. Case closed. There is no court of appeals.

Secondly, you must realize that God has established only one penalty for sin, no matter how slight that sin may seem to the sinner. Romans 6:23 *For the wages of sin is death----*

Not the physical demise of the body which comes to sinner and saint alike, but the far more agonizing second death reserved only for those who refuse to believe in Jesus Christ as their savior. While the agony of the first death only lasts for a short time, the agony of this second death is eternal, and the agony of the first death pales in comparison.

While you may forever doubt during your temporary existence on this earth, on judgment day all doubt will be erased as you stand in the presence of Christ, the son of God. At that moment, you will become painfully aware of the enormous depth of the bliss that could have been yours; and you will also realize that from that very moment, it can never be. The anguish caused by that realization of what could have been will remain in the forefront of your consciousness for eternity as you reside in the depths of hell.

THIS NEED NOT BE! God has good news for you.

In the remainder of Romans 6;23 We discover that God has provided an alternative to the execution of your sentence. -----*but the gift of God is eternal life through Jesus Christ our Lord.* By allowing his only begotten son Jesus Christ, who lived a sinless life as a man and therefore had no sin debt to pay, to suffer the anguish of this second death in your stead, God releases you from the obligation of your sins. It is now up to you to decide whether or not to believe in his promise. God is offering the gift of a free pardon but you must reach out in faith and accept it.

Advertisers bombard us through the mail and the internet with offers of free gifts. (dial 1-800-xxx xxxx to receive your free gift) The gift is there, it is obtainable to all who desire it, but you don't get it if you don't make the call. It is the same way with God except that his free gift is indeed free, with no hidden strings attached.   You don't have to buy a whatsit or attend a boring seminar.   All you need do is make the call!   You don't even have to go to church to do it.   God will hear you from where you are right now.   I will say this though, once you make the call, you will have a desire to go to church.   I accepted Christ on my front porch, but I couldn't wait until the next Sunday to go to church and make my confession of faith.   I have never looked back; I have never experienced any regret.

If you can agree with all that I have said so far, there remains only one more step.

Romans 10-9   *That if thou shalt confess with thy mouth the Lord Jesus, and shalt believe in thine heart that God hath raised him from the dead, thou shalt be saved.*

You are now ready to confess Jesus as your savior.   This confession is also called by many a profession of faith.   You are stating to yourself, to the world, and most importantly to God that you have absolute faith that he can and will deliver the promised salvation as stated in his word.   While this confession is made with your mouth, it must come from deep in the heart.   You must be prepared to forsake all pursuit of evil, and surrender to God's will.   This does not mean that you must never sin again.   As long as your soul resides in its imperfect human envelope, you will still make mistakes.   Your repentance and confession have redeemed your eternal soul, and nothing can change that.   You must, however, still contend with the devil's enticements.   To quote the words of Christ: "the spirit is willing but the flesh is weak".   To quote him again, speaking to the believers: "you have an advocate with the Father".   Christ is our defense attorney, and he has never lost a case.

After I was saved, it seemed that I sinned much more than I used to!   Actually, my sins were not more frequent, I was just a lot more concerned about them than before. The difference was that the sins that I used to enjoy, I did not want to do anymore.   I had repented! If that is your present attitude, then nothing can stand in your way.

Quoting directly from the words of Jesus: *He who comes to me, I will no wise cast out.*

See you in heaven!